# THE RUNT OAK

## TALES FROM OVER DAR

RAYMOND PILARCZYK

1st edition 2025

ISBN Paperback: 979-8-9994099-2-8
ISBN Hardcover: 979-8-9994099-3-5
Library of Congress Control Number: 2025914292

For all the sons and daughters of Vovk

# Introduction

In my backyard, I have a Live Oak tree. To merely call it a Live Oak would be an understatement. The tree is a huge Live Oak and offers shade to the entire yard and extends over the roof of the house. When one drives towards my small rural town, this tree can be visible over a mile away, since my house rests on the highest hill in the county. Again, the tree is rather large. Now, I heard some oaks can live as much as 300 to 500 years, and even on very rare occasions, 1000 years. I am hesitant to say how old this tree might be, but from stories in the town, it seems to have been here since time immemorial. Older generations where I live mention how, as children, they tried to climb the tree, but many had a difficult time getting past the trunk to even reach the lowest branches to grab onto. I think the most adapt climber of the oak in my lifetime was a cat I have. When he was a kitten, he somehow threw caution to the wind and made it far up onto the upper branches. Well, it took all day to get him down from the tree, and even a firefighter would have been equally hard pressed to accomplish this task with all the equipment at their disposal. It is a big tree and a magnificent one at that. I have come to call it the Grandmother Tree, because of its size and age. There is a noble quality and wisdom about the tree, for the shade it casts has held its reign for centuries. 'Centuries', just saying the word encompasses a lot, and this tree has surely seen a lot. From the first European settlers to the sedentary Amerindians who gave way to the advancing Plains Amerindian horse culture, this tree has endured the rise and fall of nations.

Changing of nations, the changing of time, the experiences of the tree's existence must have been like multiple worlds, far removed from those before and those that followed. The differences which mark the years it has existed could easily offer the same impression of different dimensions all to themselves. It is safe to say, this tree has made me contemplate a lot, and from this contemplation came the origins for the book "The Runt Oak". If time is just man's creation and does not really exist, are these just different dimensions in some paradox we do not understand? From the primal seed of this oak to the manifestation of our modern technological age, it has been a witness. When I mention the primal and the modern age of technology, I am not discussing just the advancement of tools from the flinthead to the computer, but how it affects the social thought process of the world too. The degree of closeness or detachment between people, whether past or present, is examined. How human or how machine-like humankind has become, because how we communicate affects how we think and feel. How human, but now with disorders, because we are not machines but humans. This, at least to me, is evident in how removed we are from nature now. Nature is content being; well… it's natural, while humanity is becoming more artificial. It is no wonder there is so much insecurity in society because of a lack of sincerity or even a prolonged trust to reveal the individual in a programmed world, that is more like a computer chip with preset expectations of acceptance. To fit in, which results in being controlled not by one's own inner being, but by the masses being led by some eerie narrative, all are accepting without question. Not prompting a conspiracy as much as questioning, budding a contemplation which the oak tree grew in me.

Ok, I have often been accused of going on tangents, but I disagree. I enjoy taking the scenic route while remaining mindful of my destination. I could go on about this oak, time, and dimensions, but that is not necessary. Why is it unnecessary? I wrote this book so I would not have to, and explaining everything according to my interpretation would remove the reader's own, which is just as relevant as mine. This is no computer program, and individual feelings and thoughts are as valid as they are desired. I have given you the foundation of this proverbial house called a book, so walk on in and sit where you like… or you do not have to sit at all, and just walk to any room you please and feel free to walk outside on the veranda if it so pleases you. Also, if I were fortunate enough to have embedded any magic into this story, I am not about to explain everything to fit the logical constraints of a computer and make it disappear. I will, though, share one more thing before you start reading. You will see my use of an extended line between paragraphs within the chapters ahead. I will show you one now…

See that? It means you just shifted from one world to another, which is coexisting at the same time. That's funny, is it not? I just said 'time', which is kind of hypocritical after all I said with my abstract thoughts concerning dimensions. So, enough, chapter one awaits you. And when I say you, I say that with respect and acceptance because YOU matter. A good story is interesting, and life would be rather boring if we were all the same. Even all trees are different down to each leaf, unique in their own right.

"Respect is not measured by how far you come, but by what you had to overcome."

# Chapter 1

# GIVE THE DOG A BONE

# The Runt Oak

*A heartfelt colorful yarn, it just becomes a matter of untangling that warmth which has been bundled up inside over the years. Patience, yes, we must have patience because this yarn did not become tangled overnight, nor was it done with ill intent. I can still see the colors, and instead of being upset over their soft nature, which has bound them into knots, let's follow them to their release by unraveling the colors according to their harmony. The colors point the way out by the way they go inward. Red, orange, yellow, and all the wonderful, vibrant variations of this, that, and those. This, that, and those. This, that, and those. Tick tock, tick tock...*

Tick tock, tick tock, went the grandfather clock. A young boy of this world sat on a stool before a wise old clock of the Old World, lost in thought. The reflection of the chimes revealed a beach on an island in his head, or was it a mountain top, or was it just somewhere, anywhere, just far away from the confines of an ordinary space for the hero to be just that, a hero. The wind blew and sent his assorted garments and baggy pants triumphantly in movement as his stern gaze under the turban surveyed his adversary. Three heads and an unruly disposition. Reaching for his scimitar, the hero went about dispatching his foe. Off went a head! Off went another head! And then… the last head fell off by itself. This would not do, for the hero did not bring a magician on this adventure to aid him.

The boy's inability to make the clay adhere to the complex task of Claymation—crafting three extended necks with enough support for the monster he was inspired to create—stopped his imagination. This was a skill which he marveled at from the Saturday morning

# Give The Dog A Bone

Sinbad movies he was so fond of. The red and orange had the color blue replace the desired yellow, so to speak, and the boy's daydreaming then had the outside raindrops upon the top story of the house's windows interrupt the rhythm of the transcendental clock. The wind blew outside as the rain pattered against a window, and the boy lost the sunny, exotic land where he would rather be.

This slight break, shoving him back into reality, caused his dog, which was lying close by, to wake in recognition, sensing this change in the boy's state of being. Ian, not Sinbad, was his name in this reality he didn't ask for, and his loyal dog, Sam, always wanted to be where Ian was. Ian was having a hard time concentrating on this or that because of those things which always seemed to bother him.

Sam looked at Ian, looking up at the familiar shape of his companion from behind. One could say, look, but that would not be altogether true. Because Sam, being a dog, sensed Ian no differently than he could smell the aged Southern house's old wood furniture, which gave comfort. Sam smelled the wood and the forest they came from, though he had never acquainted himself with those trees. Sam did not look at Ian as much as he felt Ian, though he did not know Ian when Ian was just a pup. Yes, a pup, because a dog does not see a difference in man or dog, but just part of the pack- his pack. Though he had not entered this world when Ian was younger, he could feel his friend's life just like those trees which came before. Oh, the wisdom Sam could impart to Ian, calming his inner monsters regardless of their number of heads, willing or not, and others in his adopted pack if he could only speak out loud their strange tongue.

People often think animals are not intelligent because they do not speak as we do, but that is a poor conclusion to draw. As the author Mark Twain once said, "Why would I want to know another language and say the wrong thing differently?" Twain liked animals and had even stated if he had a choice, he would rather go to dog heaven. Sam would have liked Twain, and I think Ian would have, too. Maybe Twain would have even given Ian some clever anecdote on how to stick with this and that, without those things impeding his liberating imagination.

Ian got up from his chair, and in unison, Sam got up with his tail going into automatic wag mode. Ian extended his arms and stretched. After all, a hero's work is hard work—even if he had only sat and watched his death-defying accomplishments from afar. Sam proudly extended his front legs to join the stretch while he kept wagging his tail, even though it's hard to see the little snub of a tail on a Scottish terrier. Ian walked out of the room, which housed the grandfather clock, on his way to his bedroom. Leaving the room, he could still smell the roast from that evening's supper and the voices of his mother and his Uncle Jake downstairs in the kitchen. Sam followed and could still smell: the roast, the onions, the carrots, the potatoes, peach pie, the coffee, Ian's mom's hand lotion, Uncle Jake's dirty socks, and Uncle Jake's dog Wilbur- though Wilbur was still in another county at Uncle Jake's house. Sam had never met Wilbur, but he had smelled him well enough, and smelling is knowing in dog ways.

Ian walked into his room and turned his attention to the little clay figures he had created on his dresser. There it was, the problematic Cyclops, with the unwilling head which needed his attention. Rummaging through the assorted things in a room which resembled a captain's cabin on a ship (with its books, maps, and a globe for good measure of investigation next to a telescope) he found his clay in their little plastic bags along with their tools. Ian opened up one of the plastic bags of clay and sighed. Sam, for emotional support, let out a wince of a yawn.

A dejected Ian turned to Sam with his fingers all sticky with the red clay, "How am I going to have a proper Cyclops with this to work with? This clay is too dry again. Guess we are going to have to dig up some more from the yard if this rain ever stops." Sam nodded in determined agreement, but then his head turned from Ian when he heard Uncle Jake call his name from downstairs, "Sam, Sam, come down here!" "Well, what are you looking at, Sam? Go down there and see what he wants, we can't do anything tonight with this", said Ian, like a captain who just decided there was no use putting up the sails. Sam turned his head to the side again, looking at Ian, still engaging in dog talk conversation, thinking, "Isn't wet clay what we're looking for?" Ian squatted down and cuddled Sam's head. "Go, Sam, before my mom finds a reason to call me, too. I'll be here. I'm not going anywhere; I never go anywhere. Go, boy, it's alright." Sam pressed up next to Ian's knee and then took off to see what Uncle Jake wanted.

Sam scuttled down the hall on his way downstairs. Being a dog, he had a much different perspective on this path than a human would. The doorways to the adjoining rooms to his left looked up like columns, as if he was moving down some ancient Greek or Egyptian temple which he had seen in one of Ian's books. Awe, Ian's books, which littered his room. Ian's room was rather cluttered, and Ian hated to mark his pages by bending the edges, so there was always a library of books with open pages on the floor set as backdrops for potential stages for his clay creations. One night, Sam would sleep on the Acropolis of Athens, or the next, Stonehenge. Sam knew ancient architecture well, and, it's worth noting, dogs also have imaginations.

Sam timidly approached what he never liked very much, the stairs. He looked down as the light from downstairs illuminated his far-off destination, almost like a city finally visible after a long journey from one of Ian's movies. This was different, however; he wasn't safely nestled with Ian in bed, and this apparition was real. There are no handrails for dogs, and this dog's legs hardly qualified as legs past the visual of his fur, which covered them. People often look at pyramids and never realize how difficult they are to climb, having no rails and losing all perspective on the way up. Most people slowly crawl up the pyramid as opposed to walking, which would suit the god kings just fine, awaiting them on top. Sam, though, was going down, and that meant one brisk descent to safety. Once his little legs started, there was no going back. Gravity was the force behind the courage, and inertia was his guide. Forget thinking, and there was no time for imagination, which would gladly only create a worse scenario. With his head down, saying, "one Mississippi, two Mississippi, three Mississippi," and with a flick of his furry mustache as he took a deep breath, he was off. For such a short distance, and the stairs forcing his speed to increase, it still always seemed an eternity. And just as this explanation of Sam's dilemma seemed to carry on and on, he thankfully found himself at the bottom of the stairs before one could finish reading it.

As Sam felt the security of the hardwood floor and the soft texture of the rug (some aunt of a godmother of some cousin had bought some years back) in the dining room leading to the kitchen, he heard the all-familiar banter between Uncle Jake and Ian's mom. "You know he never respected or even attempted to acknowledge our family history, or even try, Vivian?" said Uncle Jake, as he glanced at the shadow of Sam entering the kitchen. Sam had heard this conversation once before between the two, more than once, just as Ian had. It was a conversation which never materialized into any resolution between the two, which is exactly why it kept reappearing. It reminded Sam of bad weather, which also never materialized. Dark clouds and flashes of lightning would go off in the distance, and then miles away would drift away with a bunch of fanfare for nothing.

"Jacob Cyrus Higgins, do you really have to go down that path again? I don't know what is worse anymore, talking about my ex-husband, the obscure reference to a long-gone Civil War, or worse…. both," said Vivian with a vexed demeanor which brought more smiles than irritation. Uncle Jake smiled, and the sight of Sam brought everyone back to the reality of the here and now in the kitchen. "My boy, my boy", said Uncle Jake in his best Elvis impersonation. Then, from under the kitchen table where he sat, he pulled out a huge bone. "Look what I saved for you, Sam," said Uncle Jake, glowing. Ian's mom looked at Jake and the bone, which seemed bigger than Sam, and said, "Really? You kept that greasy, dirty bone under the table this whole time, while putting on airs with your long-winded lecture about society and my personal life? This is about as bad as when you once lectured me about holding a teacup wrong… when we were both drinking out of a straw, and I was 12."

Jake did a dignified cough out of spite, which also brought more smiles than irritation by its out-of-place seriousness. Vivian smiled, trying to respond with the same dignity she used earlier with even less fruitful results, "and where, may I pray tell, did you get that monstrosity from the prehistoric age?" "Lou's BBQ, I believe, about two days ago. My dog Wilbur, whom I had taken along, must have taken it out of the bag unbeknownst to me while I was driving. Just look at it, can see now why he could not sneak it out of the car," said Jake, laughing. Sam took the bone from Uncle Jake, which resulted in the bone dropping Sam and his jaw to the floor with a thud. "Bless his heart", said Vivian, as she moved towards Sam before Jake's outstretched arm gently obstructed her help. "He is stronger than you think, Viv," said Jake. "But look at him, look at that bone!" said Vivian. "Looks can deceive, sis, and runts are always stronger than they look- and why they survive," said Jake affectionately. Sam then miraculously lifted the bone from the floor. "Well, I'll be, but..." Vivian began, but Jake interrupted her again, saying, "And you will let it be and be amazed."

Vivian's slender frame glided around Jake and the table and to the back door. She opened up the door and looked outside, and wiping away a tear from Jake's last sentiments, looked down at the comical Sam holding a bone bigger than him, "the rain has stopped Sam, best you secure that prize of yours and take care not to track too much mud on your way back." Sam strained as he carried the bone with conviction for the door, doing his best not to show any difficulty, which might tarnish the grand words Uncle Jake had lavished on him. Ian's mom turned on the porch light, and she and her brother watched Sam venture out into the semi-darkness of the backyard to hide his bone for later.

Watching Sam, Uncle Jake chuckled, "You know it was lemonade and not even tea in that teacup." Vivian smirked, "Yes, I know, and you are the proper gentleman. That is the only reason I let you carry on about Greg, because you stick to the packaging and not the content, which caused me to leave him." Jake, seeking a positive spin on his sister's reconciliatory words, interjected, "He did buy you and Ian a lot." "Yes, all those books which fascinate Ian, all that knowledge of the world, but never anything about himself. He gave nothing of himself to me either, just a load of… never mind, the thing about living in a house which is a family heirloom is that you feel your long-gone relatives are always critiquing you… and expecting proper etiquette from their forever Southern Belle," said Vivian in a serious but jovial tone. "Then I will say it. There is so much bull… seems I can't say it either with them looking on- and I don't even live in this house anymore," said an apprehensive Jake. Brother and sister were silent and then both laughed, staring out into their own space, removed from their yard but towards memories all their own. "Don't take too long, Sam!" yelled Vivian out into the darkness, as the door to the backyard closed and the squeak of the screen door followed close behind.

It was quiet except for the sound of drops of rain still dripping from the roof, the sound of crickets, and all the odd sounds which one can never place but common on a summer night- which also now included the rustle of Sam as he made his way around his domain, looking for a proper spot to stash the bone.

# Chapter 2

# THE RUNT OAK

# The Runt Oak

Sam's ears perked up at the sound of the screen door, which finally closed, always taking its sweet time closing on the porch. At first, he was cautious not to drop the large bone which Uncle Jake had given. You understand, Sam did not want to give any credit to Uncle Jake's not-so-flattering words, calling him a 'runt', and above all, lumping his dear Ian into this simmering pot of pity. Uncle Jake meant well, but he always took things too far. Sam realized these two-legged dogs lacked subtly with their need to talk out loud. Humans, for whatever reason, could not see or smell as well as he, to afford such efficient communication.

Staring through the darkness from the edge of the weathered old wooden fence line which encircled the yard, Sam looked back with an expression of disenchantment at the porch under its soft yellow light, dropping the giant bone with relief. Not that the bone was just heavy, but the slick texture of it made it hard to grip as well. Sam's instincts then kicked in and emphasized that this was not just any bone, but 'his' bone he had to protect. He could still taste its surface on his mouth, and the smell of the bone marrow coursed through his veins as if in his very own blood.

There was no time to lose. Who knows what thief or criminal watched him while he foolishly focused on the door and Uncle Jake's behavior? It would be just like Uncle Jake to mean well, but go too far, to take too much time, and put his very gift in jeopardy by his antics. Sure, he was only standing by the door momentarily, but just because he was saying nothing in human thought, didn't mean he was not unconsciously complaining about the promise he had made to cut the grass in quiet canine vernacular. "Uncle Jake, you long-winded buffoon!" In dog talk, an agitated Sam said it, which another dog blocks away could have silently heard. "Oh, no, Sam!" said Sam to himself in a panic. "Now you let all the other dogs in the neighborhood know about this prized bone."

Sam was on a mission, and once Sam set his mind to something, he got it done. Tonight was different somehow, and he could smell it in the air and by his actions. When he was staring out the back door of the porch, it was something which was totally out of his character. Whether he decided to physically act or stand vigilant to protect, when Ian was young and had asthma, you could count on Sam. Ian's father always had the opinion that the asthma did not exist and it was all in Ian's head. Greg would always conveniently make such assumptions after the attraction of the moment was gone, and one of the reasons he and Vivian did not work out. "It is in your head, and you are just weak. You need to eat more" was just some of his favorite lectures to Ian. Sam knew better. He felt with all his dog senses that something was wrong beyond his friend doing it because of a poor diet. The worst one Ian's dad would turn to when he was in a rush, "the boy just wants attention. Don't you dare give it to him, Vivian," but of course Vivian did, and why Ian is still with us in this story. Greg was selfish and, for lack of a better word, was lazy. Uncle Jake would carry on, while Greg would stop short.

Sam lifted his head and started smelling across the fence line, through the long grass which Jake had promised to cut. He could smell the summer air, the rain which had moved on, and all the trees in the yard which would serve as the best marker to dig and bury- he also still smelled Uncle Jake's dirty socks, the sign of a bachelor who was not too interested in keeping up with his laundry. Hackberry trees braced, or rather secured, the fence line. Vivian hated this, but Greg never got around to removing them because he never found someone who he could pay to do it for him (and hackberries are stubborn and their disposition can be a little prickly). In the end,

Greg would just say he left them because they would secure the foundation of the fence- the same excuse when he would not replace the siding on the old house, claiming the paint would hold it together. Now, all Sam could smell was hackberry trees, because they have a way of being resilient and had taken over. It was dark, and with so many hackberry trees, it would be hard in the days to follow to remember which one he buried it under. Then Sam turned to the ideal spot, but a spot which he was always suspicious of. Sam turned to the oak, the little oak in the yard, which never seemed to get much bigger.

Every year, this mutt of a tree looked like it was on its last limbs but somehow survived. It was not just that, but it was strange in a peculiar way. It smelled different, unlike other oaks, and it had a vibration of energy around it, for lack of a better description. Although a human might not have sensed these things, Sam certainly did—though often his two-legged pack members swore someone was watching them when their backs were turned to the little oak. Sam was now facing that odd oak, and when on a mission, one must do what one must do to get it done. Readjusting the large bone he had been carrying, Sam walked over to the center of the yard where the oak existed. I say it existed because, again, it seemed to do more than just occupy its space in the yard.

Sam came up to the little oak. If Uncle Jake had to label one thing as a runt, this tree qualified. When its growth had seemed stunted, Greg, instead of having it pulled out (which probably would have been his responsibility), said just to light it on fire after he gave up on a tree house, he was building two hours into the idea, but Vivian would have none of that. Ian got his vivid imagination from his mother, and Vivian could imagine the house catching on fire, along with a sect of druids showing up. Her husband's unreliability in checking the fire would cause them to be blamed for all the other houses catching fire, along with any curses attributed to the druids.

# The Runt Oak

The steadfast little oak must have been proud of its tenacity, of annually denying its decimation, and Sam could feel its proud presence. Oaks are wise because of their life span compared to other creatures, but this one always felt wise beyond its years despite its young age. Sam started digging in front of the oak, and its unique smell became even more apparent as he got deeper. As mentioned, the bone's size and Sam's short legs made this an arduous task for the little terrier. Sam had had the courage before to hide some bones under the oak, but never to dig this deep. Sam became a little nostalgic, as well as excited. Many times, he had buried bones in the general vicinity, but for whatever reason, half the time they disappeared. This strange phenomenon he felt was the dirt settling with the extensive root system an oak usually has, so he expected he might just come across past treasures which had become more settled in the dirt. So, Sam dug, and he dug. Sam felt a little trepidation, because he was getting deeper than his body might then get out of.

Suddenly, there was a shift in the dirt, and an expanse opened up before him which seemed to lead inward. Great! There was a hole pre-dug just for him that something like a mole must have once accomplished- but how far did this hole go? Then there was a whisk of air, which blew the fur above his eyes. "That is strange?" thought Sam to himself. It had been rather still after the rain, and not only was this an unexpected breath of air, but it was fresh and not dank. The 'energy' that the oak usually exuded then felt more intense. Sam started digging around the edges of this past hole to allow room for his bone, and then suddenly the edges caved in on their own. Sam felt a pull. This energy now had intent, and it was pulling him inward! This energy also had a new sensation. It felt warm. Sam panicked, something he never did, which Ian could attest to when Ian had had one of his asthma attacks and Sam had to get Vivian. Sam spun his short body to go back from which he came, but it was too late. The force sucked him in, and it was going ever inward and not deeper- but upward! The smell of elm trees suddenly filled the air, along with assorted leaves from various trees, trees which were not found in his backyard.

A light then illuminated within the hole, it becoming more of a tunnel- or dare I say, a portal. Sam made out the leaves distinctly, which he had smelled blowing past him, as he was now being carried off the ground floor. This was the stairs' ordeal all over again, but far more extreme. Shades of warm color surrounded him, and as he moved faster, they became brighter, but this was not daytime… or had he been digging so long, morning had arrived. Then it became momentarily dark, and the air changed to smells of vegetation he had never known before. Sam could identify most of the trees, but the scent was more sweet than bitter, unlike trees in their stoic nature usually exude.

It all then drastically slowed down, and Sam could see a light appear after a slight turn in the moving passage. Sam could then feel the ground below him as he stood beneath an opening in the earth. Sam brushed off the dirt as he climbed up into the radiant light above him. What he saw when he got to the surface amazed him. He no longer had the bone, having must have lost it in all the commotion- and he certainly was not in his backyard anymore.

# Chapter 3

# SO MANY ANSWERS WITHOUT AN ANSWER

# The Runt Oak

Extraordinary! Extra, extra beyond ordinary. The extraordinary circumstance unfolded before him. Sam found himself among an assortment of trees in what looked like a clearing with the sun filtering through. The clearing was idyllic; the clearing was beautiful. Rows of trees braced the perimeter, and in front was a broad open path which extended through the foliage. Sam shook himself off some more and, surveying the surrounding ground, saw interlocking shadows which formed a surface grid of elaborate designs. Turning to see what lay behind him, he saw the hole which he had come out of and a wall of bark. Sam stepped back, and looking up from his small height, could still only see bark. He stepped back even more, but only an expanse of bark was still to be seen. Sam turned and ran forward for a stretch, then turned back around where the tapestry of shadows ended. He looked, and before his eyes was the largest tree he had ever seen- a Live Oak, to be exact. It encompassed his entire view, the biggest and most majestic tree one could imagine.

Astonished, Sam slowly walked closer in complete awe. Then he felt an energy, the same energy he was familiar with when close to the little runt oak in his backyard. It was the same, but more assertive, more mystical than mysterious. Sam then felt good, a kind of good one feels when they are next to an older person who shares a comfort endowed by experience. Answers without questions, and answers to questions, which made his past knowledge more concise.

Being a dog, this sensation was not foreign to Sam. Unbeknownst to man, the Creator has given animals the reasons for being, and that's why they are so confident in their own being, but these reaffirmations given to him now were more detailed in the how and why, more than Sam ever imagined. If you wanted to know 'why the chicken crossed the road?' Sam not only understood but also felt the reasons. One could say Sam now understood the reasons for the road's construction—and much more—to give you a small idea of his experience.

This was unbelievably insightful, but also downright unnerving to know so much about so much, in so little time. Sam walked around the trunk of the grand old oak till panting, he found himself at the very hole from which he had escaped earlier. This place where he found himself was spectacular, but he then thought the smart thing to do was to find the one way back and report to Ian and his mom what he had found. Hesitation then gripped Sam as he remembered his journey through the hole.

There would be no counting down with the state of Mississippi, for that would give him enough time to think of a reason not to go through it again. Alas, there did not seem to be another way, and Sam was not about to walk around the circumference of this humongous oak again. It also then occurred to him that if he did not retrace his way back to his yard at this very moment, this unusual hole could just as easily disappear. Why not? Everything else here seemed more than unusual. And he did not ask it in dog talk too loudly, because he was afraid this place would probably give him the answer. Explanations are often explained here, apparently. This would open up a whole new can of worms, and the only worms he wanted to be acquainted with were the ones he left in the soft, wet dirt outside the hole back home. With this secretly in mind, as not to tempt more answers to things which he did not want to know, Sam simply counted to one and said, "Georgia."

Sam jumped forward into the hole. He was grateful, for he currently had a running start, and the pulling energy of before had not come forth yet. He was then not grateful, because he ran into a barrier. In the darkness, Sam smelled and felt what was holding him back. Beyond this obstruction, he also felt that exuberant energy which he was expecting. The obstruction turned out to be roots, oak roots to be exact, and they were vibrating at an incredible rate. Sam then, in frustration, thought of a bad word he once heard Ian's dad say- when, once, a premature venture to move the BBQ pit had sent the heavy grill off and onto Greg's toe. This impulsive attempt at vulgarity did not help the situation.

Instantly, it made sense. Again, this ever-flowing knowledge of this place made its influence known, and he even knew where the energy was coming from, now being right under it. The energy was being produced from the large oak tree.

This was enough education for Sam, and he bolted back outside of the hole. Sam then shrugged, perplexed by this predicament. How was he going to get home, and if he found a way, would this place or tree let him? Now trees have their pecking order as they say down South, and the hierarchy this tree would fall under could be no less than royalty. Sam humbly bowed his head, with all the humility of his already short frame could muster. While also trying to mask his fear, Sam inquired in his overloaded mind if this king would be as if so kind to show him a way home. The response was this: the tree slightly beckoned Sam toward the path he saw upon entering this strange place. Sam did not know if it told him or if it nudged him with energy, but it revealed that the way was down that path outside of the forest clearing. What was Sam to do?

A gentle baritone voice from within Sam said, "The way out is away from the way in," or rather, from a voice that was not his. "Just great. I was getting all these answers, and now it is feeding me riddles," thought Sam. There was a soft rustle in the branches above him as if to say, "tisk tisk, youngin." Sam turned with slight irritation at this suggestive remark, but then felt oddly ashamed.

# So Many Answers Without An Answer

Wisdom, this tree had wisdom, and if one were to think of the extended wisdom of the runt oak in relation to its size, this mighty oak increased it by its size way past comprehension. We must also note that the use of one's intelligence, not the amount of it, determines wisdom. This was wisdom, and it was sure of itself, wanting no arguments from Sam. Then Sam felt the words, "You humbly asked, but it was your respect for your elders which prompted my willingness." Sam, being from the South, knew about manners, or at least a token show of respect, and this noble tree had spoken. As mentioned, it also reminded him of royalty, and there was no shortage in the tales of old that Ian read to him of kings just as quickly ruling severe punishment as they did generosity. Sam then thought it best to follow the advice, though the directive was far from the direction he wanted to go- before his disobedience caused a branch to fall on him and end the conversation altogether. "Ok, ok… I mean yes, your gracious majesty," said Sam, walking down the path which lay in front of him.

As Sam headed out of the clearing along the path, he felt the large tree's energy subside, and something else—all those voices, beyond the usual explanations of creation he knew from home— faded as he left the tree. It became obvious that this phenomenon of knowledge had also come from the tree.

When he stepped out from the giant oak's shadow, everything felt almost normal. Sam was now at least familiar with his current state of senses, though the brilliance of this place he could not yet place. Unlike when he stared at Vivian and Jake on the porch, stalled by some foreboding pause, he now moved forward as the same dog he always had been, purpose in motion. Whatever he might come across, he did not know, but whatever found him would find the authentic Sam, he knew himself to be.

# Chapter 4

## UNCLE AMOS IS A GLOW

# The Runt Oak

"I say, boy, they're called colors, I say, colors!" said a voice startling Sam, as he looked about for the source which was addressing him. Sometimes it's hard to place a voice in a forest, and who knows the dynamics of hard-to-place voices in the odd place Sam now found himself. Sam picked up his head, which was lost in thought, when the voice first became apparent. Stopping, he looked around, and from out of the bushes came a large armadillo. A strange armadillo, like everything else that seemed a little fantastical here- with a pipe in his mouth, of all things. The armadillo came forward and said again, "I say colors, boy, colors." Sam stopped in his tracks and said, "You can speak in human talk?"

At this moment, another thing struck Sam; he too spoke out loud like a human by his own reactionary response. "What boy? I say, of course you can talk, you're talking now, ain't ya? What? A cat got the dog's tongue?" said the armadillo in a Southern drawl. "As I was saying, them dar are colors you be a seeing." The mystery of why this place looked so brilliant was answered. "You're just used to black and white, since I sense you are not from around here- but the places found below the Grandfather Tree. Oh, my deepest apologies, I have not introduced myself. Salutations, I say, greetings, my name is amiss… no it's not, for I know it well… I mean I say Amos, Uncle Amos around these here parts, and I have been waiting fer ya son," said the armored covered gentleman.

Sam did not know what to say, but his name was not amiss either: "My name is Sam." "Well, of course it is, boy", said Uncle Amos with mirth. Sam got his thoughts together while the armadillo just stood there with a twinkle of satisfaction in his eye. "Where am I? Why can't I get back the way I came? Why…," said Sam. At this, Uncle Amos cut him off with a laugh, saying in a condescending tone, "Good Lord, son, all these 'whys', don't tell me you are bumfuzzled again, I say bumfuzzled." Sam stopped and looked down, and then looked up at the armadillo, as a puppy might after it got in trouble. "There will be plenty of time, boy, I say, yes, der will! But now I have someone you need to meet, and no time to waste. Allow me to go fetch her ladyship from the bushes… and I say, boy, don't be bumfuzzled in her presence, because time is of the essence and she cannot be in the sunlight for long." "Is she the queen of this place?" inquired Sam. "She be but a Lady, and I'm not talking about some woman you meet getting your crackerjacks at the general store, but that be a queen… though you know the way her kind wander about, don't cha? They reckon not to call anyone of them a queen for the sake of free roaming propriety, but I say she is the queen and remember that", said Uncle Amos with reverence.

Sam obeyed as a proper ambassador of his breed and followed behind the armadillo. All the while, Uncle Amos' backside waddled back and forth while he left a scent of vanilla from his pipe behind him, which caused Sam to cough. "He be bumfuzzled again," said Uncle Amos out loud to himself, as he then beckoned Sam to stop. The armadillo then disappeared into the bushes and then reappeared, as a soft light made his return known- this light came from above his nose.

Sam slowly approached Uncle Amos as the armadillo quietly motioned for Sam to come forward. Looking down on Uncle Amos' nose, Sam saw a soft glow pulsating under a little parasol. "Come closer, little one, don't be afraid, such behavior does not suit your character," said a far but distant voice which rang like church bells on a Sunday. "Be careful of the sunlight, my ladyship," said Uncle Amos with tenderness. "Please, Amos, dispense with all the titles.

# The Runt Oak

All life is just as important as any other. My name is Gloria, and we have been waiting for you, Sam," said the heavenly voice as she lowered the ornate parasol. As the voice revealed itself, Sam swore he heard a choir singing at a frequency only his kind could detect. Below was a glowworm, but somehow much more, and Sam felt good all over. Sam felt the kind of good as when you feel safe, when you are with someone who understands and listens. Now, though, it became Sam's turn to listen with all the senses a dog may call upon- and with an endearing softness, this is what the angelic glow worm said:

"Welcome to our realm. I do not have a name for our realm, because that would be selfish of any one people to feel they are entitled to give a title to everything all experience. My name is Gloria, and there is no need for anymore, for those I care for and return my compassion use Gloria- and I care for everyone to my best ability. Look around you, young one; don't you feel these people suffering? "

Sam looked around and saw no people, and looked again to make sure his senses had not failed him, but could find no people. At this reaction, the word bumfuzzled could be heard escaping from under the nose which held Gloria. There was a breeze that then said "shhhhhh" in unison with a momentary rise of light from Gloria. Uncle Amos felt ashamed and lowered his head. "Enough of that, you lovable cottonwood of an armadillo, or I might slide onto the ground", said Gloria in a lighthearted manner. The armadillo adjusted his nose back to a proper level, and before he could smile, the glow worm with a soft laugh reminded him that a grin could also cause her to fall off.

Gloria then drew Sam's attention back to her with a sparkle of light. "Yes, these people. These trees, these blades of grass, and even the rocks are people. A person is any living being, and anything with energy is a person. All is alive in their fashion, despite how enthusiastic they are about conveying this fact of existence. If not, how could you feel energy in a world comprised of black holes sapping the smiles and the tears from happening? The trees which surround you now are a perfect example, the linden trees," exclaimed Gloria.

"So that is what trees, I mean people, they are," said Sam, correcting himself. "We do not have these people in the world I am from." Sam then paused, trying to update the files in his nose with a new definition and name. "But they are in your world, my innocent one. Admittedly, your kind can smell over great distances, but not as far as your known world allows—not far enough to smell the ocean's salty tears, the blossoms on the far side of your world, or even across the mountains blocking the western winds," Gloria said. "But they look pretty happy to me. They look pretty and happy," said Sam, perplexed. "Then believe me when I say they are not, because looks can be deceiving. The linden people only use their beauty to cloak their fears and sadness, beauty being a shallow veil covering the root of the problem. Yes, their roots, their hearts buried deep in dread. You, of all people, should smell their problems and not rely on mere sight alone. I remember your people, Sam; they left our world a long time ago. A wise few still recall the day Vovk the Grey led your people from our world to yours: dogs, wolves, foxes, you Sam… all of Vovk's people."

"Why did they leave?" asked Sam. "Maybe because they could smell too much, the good and bad. You must have felt the energy of the Grandfather Tree, which courses through his roots and touches all here. Too many voices interfering with your people's need to howl in solitude, I guess," said the solemn, but somewhat vague, Gloria. Sam had a strange feeling of pride and sadness. Cocking his head to the side, Sam swore he could hear distant howls that echoed within him.

# The Runt Oak

At this, Gloria moved her parasol back over her body as she said, "My people cannot withstand the sun's rays for long, so let me impart what we need for our meeting today. Follow the path, the path by the sun, which I now must take a break from. Maybe if Vovk's people had not chosen to leave, these problems would not have grown so unnoticed till it was too late… maybe. There are words in the roots, and feelings in those words. Follow the path, and you will know what needs to be done in due time if your smell does not fail you. We here have become too blinded by sight, and why you and your nose were called back to us. Now go, son of Vovk, while the trail is still rich with its scent. And Sam, you will not be alone. Trust your senses and those who will make up your pack," said Gloria as her words faded, while Uncle Amos disappeared back into the darkness of the bushes from which he had brought her.

The armadillo then quickly returned, and in a chirpy voice said, "There you go, son, all you need to fetch the truth." Uncle Amos smiled, though it seemed a rather forced smile. "So, follow the path? That is what I was told to begin with. Follow a smell I do not know? That is just brilliant!" pouted Sam. "I say, boy, I say, that will not do. You heard her ladyship well enough. Why complex the matter? You can only do one thing at a time, son, and I don't have time to learn ya," lectured Uncle Amos- now with a genuine smile. Sam turned to the path which held the sun on its horizon, and looking around, said to himself, "Linden people?"

Sam turned back once again and said to Uncle Amos, "Will I ever see Gloria again?" Uncle Amos, preparing his pipe, looked up and said, "Smell that?" "Vanilla," said Sam. "Dang blasted boy, not the tobacky!" grumbled Uncle Amos. Sam sniffed the air again and said, "Chocolate, a touch of hibiscus, and some fruit." "Dark chocolate, to be exact, of the truffle variety, boy, I say! That is Gloria. It was not just the sun that beckoned her to leave, but her tea, you finally smelled, was getting cold. Now remember how to smell!"

## Uncle Amos Is A glow

Before Sam could respond, Uncle Amos had vanished. "Well, I might have smelled that if it was not for that confounded pipe of yours!" shouted Sam. Sam turned back to the path and started going forward again, and this time, instead of just seeing linden people, he smelled them, too.

# Chapter 5

# TALKING YOURSELF TOO FAR

# The Runt Oak

Sam walked, and he walked. He had become fully acquainted with the linden people by now. He could see why this world caused one to forget their sense of smell by all the dazzling visuals which surrounded him, but one should not ignore one's gut instincts, lest you become blinded by the narrative of a façade. Sam understood how appearances might fool one into thinking the package was the truth and not the content. Sam became very bothered by this. He couldn't deny the honey-like smell of the yellow linden blossoms once he smelled them. There had to be some hope for them, in order to exude such a suggestive scented sincerity- but there was something off, and they smelled funny. This fragrance was fragmented. The worst lies are those which take truth and then manipulate it. No matter how sweet the flowers smelled, Sam could detect a bitterness in their roots, which Gloria had warned him of. The linden said one thing, wanted themselves to believe one thing, but deep down they doubted a lot… mainly themselves. Their insecurity tainted their happiness, no matter how joyful they tried to appear.

Sam then noticed something strange about the linden; the strangeness revealed itself at the edges where they gathered. Some of the linden people felt different- felt more authentic. It would have been hard to detect if they had not been isolated from the exaggerations of the crowd. It never had occurred to Sam to actually go up and take a closer look, which is what the linden people did their best to prevent with their beauty-making, implying an 'I'm not worthy' protocol.

# Talking Yourself Too Far

Sam, though, was a dog, and going up to trees was something he did instinctively. As Sam approached one of these lindens that was removed from the group on the edges of their grove, he felt a trembling voice, "Don't you dare reconvene that deplorable tradition of Vovk's people on me, you little whimper snapper!" Sam stopped in his tracks and saw what the tree meant. Sam slowly put his back leg down, and, oddly being able to understand the silent language of the tree, said, "Sorry, just what my kind does, but I promise not to do it around here." "Good," said the tree, "this is not your territory to mark, but what little space I still have, which I can call myself, unlike those other people around me who just care what the others are told to think."

Sam then felt it, best to give this linden a little space and walked towards the other lindens grouped together. The other lindens appeared nervous, as they turned on the charm with their flowers and heartfelt leaves, saying, "Look at me, I am doing great!" Sam looked at their little clumps of yellow flowers, which trembled, and stepped back. Sam did not feel threatened by them, but this lack of sincerity made him feel uneasy. Going back to the removed linden, he felt a lot better, and it seemed the tree had become more relaxed towards him. Getting closer, Sam noticed its flowers were more like fruits, little berries to be exact. This linden actually bore fruit from what it felt, and not what it tried to portray. It still had flowers, but its beauty had meaning. This tree had something confident inside, which made it far more appealing. The silent voice then spoke again to Sam, "They are afraid of themselves, which makes them extra fearful of me. Go ahead, take some of my berries. I am not afraid to give. They only want to take, and you reap what you sow- their shallow character bears nothing to give."

Sam carefully took some berries, but then had nowhere to put them. One of the heart-shaped leaves of the linden then softly fell down on Sam's nose, and he heard, "Wrap it in this." Sam folded the berries within the leaf and placed them between one of his paws. "They are not bad people; they are just scared of being true to themselves. It is sad. Best, I am on the edge like a few others. Feeling me cry would just make their condition worse," said the isolated linden. That the other lindens appeared so beautiful, but so unhappy, made their affliction of self even more disheartening.

Sam felt for them, and the forgiving tree, which would not give up on them. The lone linden, with deep melancholy, said, "It's even worse below; fear keeps their roots from speaking, and they say nothing." Sam pressed his head against the linden, making sure not to lift any leg to frighten it, and gave it a dog hug. A dewdrop then fell on Sam's nose from above, and he felt the word "thank you." Yes, Gloria was right, there was something wrong with this place, but he did not know what he could do about it or how he would ever get back home. Sam continued along the path, leaving the grove of linden people. As he proceeded, he noticed the path to be less spacious and wilder with undergrowth. One would expect that this would make Sam feel frightened, but it did not. The trees, these people, seemed to press in close for security and not to harm. Sam felt confusion and not malice, though it made him a little uneasy if they thought he could solve their problems.

Ian would often whistle when out of sorts. Sam sensed Ian doing this whenever he was nervous or focused on uncontrollable things. As Sam walked through the heavy foliage pressing in on the path, he found himself whistling, too. This new ability elated Sam, and he became immersed in trying to replicate all the melodies Ian had shown him. The whistling also seemed to make most of the surrounding trees more at ease as well, except for a few trees, like a few people, who get irritated by whistling.

Whistling while he walked, he could hear an echo, but this echo seemed a little strange. The more complex the melodies, the more they would change upon return. They would not change for long if he kept to the same melody, but still would come back in slight variations of his initial composition, compositions by the venerated composer Ian.

Pausing, Sam attempted a whistle he always wanted to try, the sharp 'get over here' whistle. Ian always did this when outside, and it was time for them both to come back into the house, or when they would go for a walk, and Ian wanted to call him back. For Sam, it was almost like another form of his name. Sam puckered up his snout and tried to say his name in whistle talk. At first, his long tongue got in the way, but then out came a sharp whistle, breaking away from the shrill of the initial note.

Sam got goose bumps, and a powerful sense of being came over him. Calling your own name can be a humbling experience. We are so used to people always saying our name for their own motives, that when confronted with yourself calling on you for the sake of being you, well, it can be overwhelming in the empowerment it can give.

Sam stood there in a moment of glorious self-recognition. When this self-evident truth subsided, something else occurred to him. Of the whistling he had done, this was the most direct, but now there was no echo. There was not even a hint of his name. Did this world fear its own identity so much that it wouldn't even permit a whistle of self-worth? Then he heard the returning whistle, or rather a long-lost relative of that whistle, which had taken a while to return. Suddenly, there was a flurry of all the melodies he had been whistling, which came back at an accelerated rate. There was then a pause, and arriving late, the short 'calling name' of a whistle finally sounded. This time it was the same, if not with more emphasis, and was followed by the word "boring."

Sam felt some movement from the corner of his eye, and a shape bobbed from under the shadows of the branches as it started talking. Talking would be kind. This creature was chattering, and the more it chattered, the quicker it would chatter. "Boring," and then it would imitate Sam's calling whistle, laugh hysterically, and sing every melody, more or less, that Sam seemed to have been reciting from Ian's repertoire. This hyper being was hard to focus on, but it and its constant chatter were slowly coming down from the tops of the tree towards him. "Boring, ba bah boring, board me on a flight to Bora Bora. Bombastic, ecstatic, elastic, eccentric, on a wing and pa pah prayer, bu buh Buddha, positively esoteric," and then said "dynamic" as it sang all the melodies backwards. Sam got agitated. Even his patience wore thin.

Suddenly, the lowest overhanging branch revealed the source of Sam's antagonist. It was a mockingbird, doing well… mocking. Sam was no stranger to these birds; half the states in the South had this bird as their state bird. Every dog, and every cat, down to every squirrel, at least ten times in their life, had to avoid these birds swooping down on them. When not making their presence physically known, they would sing for hours on a still night. They were the nightingales of the South, with a preference for cover tunes, from Hank Williams to the sound of a lawn mower. Accustomed to their arrogant nature, Sam braced himself for the fatal swoop down, which never came. The bird hopped from one branch to another till it perched itself on a branch which was at eye-level with Sam. It was then quiet, peered closer at Sam and said… "Mim!!!" Sam jumped, and the bird started hopping around Sam in a frantic whirling dervish of oratory.

This energetic, erratic behavior seemed to last till Sam finally gave up, giving the bird any attention, and Sam simply lay down. The bird then hopped onto Sam's head and said, "Boring." Sam wanted to ignore him, but the other half of him, which the bird had baited, had something to say. "Your kind I am familiar with," said Sam with a huff. Then, with an intellectual flourish, Sam, attempting to outsmart the mockingbird, declared, "It's perfectly logical that a bird so focused on imitation would be found in a place lacking self-acceptance. Duh da do you happen to have a nah nah name?" mocked Sam again. "Mim, mah mah Mim! Told you, sa sa sold you, stole your songs, made them mah mine and in no time," said Mim the mockingbird, as it opened its wings with a flash of black and white, taking a sarcastic bow in front of Sam. "My name is Sam, and Sam is going to leave now. Have a ga ga goooooood day!" said Sam, stepping around the bird and starting down the path again. As Sam was walking away, he heard Mim whistling, and the sound was not getting any further away. Mim was following him. Sam could now understand why a select few had so much disdain for whistling.

# Chapter 6

## SHARE SHARE AND SHARE UNLIKE

# The Runt Oak

Sam kept along the path, moving ever forward to where he did not know. If Mim's presence had any saving grace, it was that it put an emphasis on Sam being told to trust his nose. The only way Sam could bear the mockingbird's ongoing barrage of noise was to put his sense of hearing on momentary hold. Sam started to identify the trees by smell before he saw them, and with that, he could also feel their roots, which had their issues just like the lindens. For instance, the elms exhibited paranoia.

Sam felt mentally and physically exhausted and found a spot to rest next to an elm that was too scared to say anything. By this time, even Mim had slowed down with his insistent banter. Sam turned to him as the bird slowly made up the distance towards him, hop by hop. "Why don't you fly?" said a tired Sam. "Fly,fa fah fly, in the sky, no want, no want to tah try," said Mim protectively. "Yes, fly, you are a bird and not just a 'person'. Wish I could fly," said Sam. "They da dah they left me that day, on the ground. Poor little Mim, so scared, so so sad, so scared, scar scarred for life, cannot fly," said Mim, and he cried.

Sam now felt horrible for unknowingly upsetting Mim. Most insecure people can be very arrogant to hide their fears, and when they break down, their real weak sense of being is even more amplified than the charade of false confidence they portray. Well, if this Mim was going to keep following him around, Sam thought it best to see if he could maybe help him. So, Sam said nothing and waited for Mim to regain his composure, and simply let him know he was there to listen.

# Share Share And Share Unlike

Sam listened often to Ian, and Sam found that Ian always found some comfort in talking to Sam. After all, being a dog, he was the perfect listener because what could he tell Ian when not being able to talk to humans and interrupt Ian's train of thought, or even worse, give him advice he did not want to hear. People usually hear what they want to hear, and Sam let Ian say what he wanted to hear. Might not have fixed the problem, but always made the problem less stressful because Ian did not have to carry the burden alone. Sam sat down on his hind legs and then felt a very timid Mim get next to him. After a moment of silence, after a moment of embracing trust, Mim was ready for a 'come to Jesus' meeting as they say down South.

We will ignore bird talk because we, Sam, and even Mim would find its translation too garbled to understand his peculiar abstract art form he called speech. Art's purpose is to ask questions of the viewer, but Sam needed answers, while Mim needed acceptance. Sam and Mim communicated in a universal sense of senses, not too removed from dog talk but just as clear. In other words, there was no mud in the water. Before we can get to this conversation from the heart, we will have to let Mim get something out of his system in his usual manner.

"Wah wah what cha got in yoyo yeah yer paw, that I saw, when you were wa wah walking. I saw, I sa saw, in your pah pah paw?" yapped Mim. "Nothing, you feathered mosquito. Stop buzzing around my belongings," scolded Sam. "Ba bah belongs, you only got one, just like there is only one sun, you are no fa fa fun. Untie that lah leaf, and sha show what it is, and wah where it's from?" begged Mim. "No!" exclaimed Sam, and he sat looking forward, not wanting to hear anymore about it. "Share and sha share alike?" said Mim quietly after a pause. "No!" said Sam, almost in a growl. Mim's immediate concerns subsided, so we can now focus on what Mim needed to say but struggled to share.

# The Runt Oak

The colors which defined this place disappeared, as grey memories came flooding back to Mim. It was a flood which his patchwork dam of uttering colorful nonsense has been doing its best to hold at bay. What Sam had in his leaf drifted away on the same current that took away what the ash wood thought about the junipers. Under this submerged ocean of fear, Mimi's tragedy floated to the surface. There was no stuttering or avoidance; the pain was self-evident.

"I woke up and found myself fluttering to the ground. I was falling and could not fly. I know I could not fly because I had seen my parents fly, and flying was something I was not doing. I was falling. I was too shocked to know where I was at first. I saw the grass but did not know what it was, because I had never seen the grass up close before. Everything was so different on the ground. Different perspectives can make things so different. The closer I was, the less I knew. I could not see through it, so I looked up at my home. From above, I saw my brother and sister falling too, though at least I thought it was them. Everything was moving so slowly and happened so fast. I then felt the presence of my parents all around, and then became sure that I saw my brother and sister fall because I heard them crying on the ground. I was so young, I did not understand our words yet, and still to this day cannot remember the words they tried to say, which we then did not know. My parents kept flying around and perching above me, as if to tell me everything was fine- everything was as it should be. My mother kept making a sharp chirping noise, a word I had not heard her say before. I finally found the courage to move. I had to move because my parents stopped going towards me, but they still seemed just out of reach. Grass, grass, and just grass, everything seemed the same. I might have gone forward, or I might have gone in circles. There was no way to tell. So many times, I think I came close to meeting one of my siblings, but it never happened. As soon as I heard my brother or sister coming closer, they would change direction to the sound of my parents, who always led them away from me to them. I just wanted to go to anyone. I felt so alone and frightened. This continued for hours, and suddenly I saw the face of my mother. She gave me a grub, and before I could plead with her to explain, she flew off."

Mim collected his courage inside and then went on. "As the sun started to go down, my father did the same, giving me something to eat. What did I do wrong? What did we do wrong? Did some danger cause my parents to push us from our home? Fear shook me; I was terrified. I then felt the brush of wings above me. It was my parents pushing me to go towards a dark, towering mass. I could hardly hop anymore till I found they had guided me under a bush. Terrified, I must have fallen asleep- because I do not remember the night till the light of day woke me up. The day started much the same as the day before, but it did not last long. This is when one of Kit's people showed up. I saw its long tail in the grass and heard its crackling 'meow' noise. I was already out in the infernal grass again and again, lost in my own tracks. I dare not move, and swear I felt the brush of its whiskers almost graze me as it quickly moved past. Then I heard a squeal. My brother or sister must have been responsible, but their yelling was too brief for certain identification. I am sure that the next cry I heard was that of my father, and I felt an enormous sound on the ground come crashing over, as I expected, the Kit person and my father were at odds. Many times, I had seen my parents chase the people of Kit from our house, but this was no game, as their chase often appeared to be. My father was fighting for his life, fighting for our lives. Why did you ever put us on the ground, Father? I cannot tell you what happened next, still cannot see past the darkness to this day. When I came to, I saw my brother. I know it was him, and he was flying, really flying, though not high. Then a dark shadow blocked out my view, and he was no more. I just stood there and could not move. I was not about to try to fly, no, I was not. I will not fly. I will not fly. Then I saw a feather blow by and lodge itself on a tall blade of grass. It was my mother's feather. I will not fly. I cannot fly. I will not fly. I will say anything, anything others say, but you will not make me fly."

The gray then faded, and the colors returned. Sam came to from the deep conversation and turned to find Mim resting against his shoulders. "Mim… Mim?" said Sam softly, "it's alright, you're not there anymore." Mim then awoke from reliving his nightmare and instantly snapped back into his frantic self. Sam knew better now and welcomed his odd behavior for the time being. It actually made Sam smile; it was much better than the petrified young bird that was afraid to move. "Sit, sat, sit, stagnant, still, still is Sam the sta sta stubborn man," said Mim in a blustery show of hyperbole, trying to push the reality of his past far back within again. Sam turned to Mim and, from his paw, opened the linden leaf. "Take some berries. A dog cannot eat these", said Sam, with a compassionate smile beneath the furry mustache which covered his nose. "Yes, yes, we are na nah not alike, not the sa sah same…" yapped Mim, till he could focus and see Sam's kind offer revealing the berries. Mim looked up at the berries appreciatively, "Sha share and share unlike."

# Chapter 7

# THROUGH THE BRAMBLES

# The Runt Oak

Flaaah-rugh, and then there was nothing. The sound of breathing with a slight wheezing could be heard. Flaaaah-rugh, flaaah-rug and everything started to pop. Pah pah pah pop pop pop pahcka pahcka packa paaaahka, kaput and it stopped. Grey smoke filled the air and clouded the boy and the machine. "I must have flooded it," said Ian with a less-than-enthusiastic stare at the push mower in the backyard. The little lawn mower was not the only thing flooded. So was Ian's mind. Since Sam had gone missing the night before, his mind had been a constant wreck. Ian found himself walking around, talking nonsense, while he had done everything he thought possible since morning to find Sam. He started whistling as he messed around with the little hose to the fuel pump on the mower.

Whistling for Ian was just another way to feel he was moving forward when things were out of his control at a standstill. Ian hated waiting for others to get the job done. All that morning, when he and his mom had scoured the yard looking for Sam, or trying to find a break in the fence where he might have gotten out, he had to listen to his mom. While Ian would whistle when he was alone to ease his anxiety, his mom did what he did when stressed in the presence of another- talk nonsense. Talk about the removed issues, which were not the ones troubling them.

This morning it was the neglected grass, and Ian thought it was just as good as an excuse as any to find something to do which he could control. Uncle Jake was good about keeping his promises, and no doubt he would show up later with his riding lawnmower to cut the grass as promised, but Ian needed something to do now. His mom protested because all the pollen in the air still brought back memories of her son's asthma attacks. Ian still had remnants of his affliction when the pollen was heavy, but he had outgrown any serious breathing threats some years ago- plus, cedar had been the main culprit, which would set off his asthma, and there were no cedar trees here since they had moved back to his mom's family house.

So, instead of hearing his mom talk about the grass while looking for breaks in the fence, Ian thought he might as well just cut the lawn himself. Instead of talking nonsense about the small-town postal service, which he had countered his mom's woes about the lawn, he would do something productive. He wanted to find Sam just like his mom, so he would cut the grass and she would clean the house.

They both had spent the entire morning calling the neighbors, calling the vet in case anyone notified them finding Sam, the dreaded local shelter, police and fire department, and taking many agonizing drives around the neighborhood when one could probably not concentrate long enough because of anxiety to recognize Sam- even if they had spotted him. Though their efforts seemed futile so far, it was better than the action Greg would have taken. Ian's father would have handled this in another way. He would blame it on someone else after a token effort to save face, and then conclude that he would just buy another dog. All of this would also only take place after Ian, or his mom, prompted his father to make a reactionary effort to silence what he considered badgering.

Ian stood looking down at the lawn mower, while not really looking at the lawn mower at all. He was still focusing on Sam and wondered if Sam was safe. Ian gazed toward a far-off place in his mind, hoping to find Sam. At this moment, he noticed a mockingbird jumping along the top of the fence line and then jumping to the ground and up again. This mockingbird was then joined by another, and both seemed rather interested in something on the ground.

# The Runt Oak

At first, Ian thought it was just the recent rain which washed all the seeds and insects to the surface, holding their interest. Ian then spotted movement in the grass. Every time one bird would go to the ground, its beak laden with morsels, it would then be empty before they came out. This seemed rather in reverse. Ian walked over to where the birds were currently causing such a commotion. As Ian got into their space, this sent both birds into a manic frenzy of sharp chuckling noises. "As expected, talk about tough love," thought Ian, shaking his head. Below on the ground was a baby mockingbird hopping through the grass, which the parents had been feeding and directing about. Ian had witnessed this before and found out from his Uncle Jake that mockingbirds kick their young out of their nest days before they can actually fly. It was just their way. Then, for over a week, the parents would spend an anxiety-filled time ensuring the survival of the fledgling till it found their wings.

"Such a strange way to raise a baby," thought Ian, but at least they knew where the baby was. Ian did not know where Sam was, and taking a cue from the mockingbird's constant beacon to their baby, he let out a sharp whistle, calling for Sam. Ian waited, but Sam did not appear. Looking at the little mower, he saw how it shuddered when running, but then remembered- he had not been able to get it started. It was just a slight vibration, but it seemed the grass vibrated too. The grass vibrated towards the little oak in his yard. Ian looked closer at the grass around the tree and discovered a large hole under it. Getting on his knees, he peered inside. "Sam?" said Ian. "Well, it won't get done like that," he heard a voice say. Ian turned over his shoulder and saw that it was Uncle Jake who had arrived with his riding mower.

"Well, it won't get done like that." Sam kept moving around the tangled vines which blocked their path, trying to find a way through them. "Won't ga gah get done like that. Won't wha wha won't. No, sir, son of Vovk," said Mim, again trying to get Sam's attention. Sam motioned for Mim to be quiet. Sam then turned sharply towards Mim in a raised voice, "There is no need to whistle in my ear! I heard you." "I did not wah whistled in your ear!" snapped back Mim. "Then who did?" questioned Sam of the bird. "Don't know, dah dah doesn't care, but you need to lah listen if we are going to ga gah get through here," retorted the equally frustrated bird. Sam paused. He definitely heard a whistle… or did he? The whistle reminded him so much of Ian, but when you miss someone, a lot of things happen which you cannot explain, which brings you back to them.

Sam and Mim had been traveling down the path since morning, and the going had not been that difficult. Now, the path was dark and obstructed by brambles before them. The jagged vines crisscrossed everywhere and had large thorns. "You keep telling me that won't do, but you won't tell me what will, you opinionated chatterbox," informed Sam to Mim. Mim started clucking and going ballistic at these words, and then quietly started hopping around Sam. Mim would hop, then stop for emphasis, and slowly start hopping again.

"See, it's really easy to judge someone till you yourself have to provide a solution," lectured Sam. "Hop, hippity hop, hop, son of Vovk, with fur like a mah mop. Hop! One must hop over these pa pah pointy arms, and not tah try to go uh under or around," said a resolute Mim. Sam looked at Mim, approached one bramble, and hopped over it. Sam then looked for a lower one going forward and hopped over that one. Mim then started to hop over a bramble with a gurgling noise of approval, seeing that Sam finally understood his consultation on the prickly matter.

Mim was right. After all, if anyone knew the benefits of hopping, it would be him. Both Sam and Mim hopped. The going was slow, but it was going. Sam started to feel tired and wanted to take a breather, but Mim would not let him. As if his subconscious was reminding him of that fateful day he lost his family, Mim said,

"When in ta tah trouble, keep hopping, standing stah still will not help ga get out of the duh darkness."

After a while, Sam found that his short terrier legs actually had a penchant for hopping- Sam just never realized this. Oh, it might have dawned on him after he found it easy to jump on furniture at his house, but Vivian never allowed him to explore that vocation for long. Sam made the best of his present situation, hopping and smiling, recalling Ian's mom saying, "Get off the furniture." About the only thing Sam still had to get accustomed to was Mim talking nonsense every so often, as the bird multitasked, hopping over the brambles and providing his verbal interjections. The hopping then became easier, as it became easier to make out where all the vines covered the path. The light was breaking through the undergrowth again- they were going to make it out of the brambles!

A hop there, and then a hop there, and then… they were free of the tangled path. If there was one redeeming quality to say about the brambles, at least those roots knew who they were. They could not help that they were born pointy with a sprawling inclination, and not once did they try to make a poignant statement to Sam other than saying, "jump a little higher here", or-"just want you to know I am over here, though you can't see me very well in the darkness because I'm crowding you." Yes, the brambles knew who they were and had helped the travelers. Guess one could say the brambles were accountable for their actions or even more commendable- taking accountability for the actions of others because of their very own existence.

# Chapter 8

## SEEING IS NOT BELIEVING

# The Runt Oak

Sam and Mim had tracked quite a distance after escaping from the congested path of the brambles, rejuvenated by the now reappearing open path. By the time the sun was setting, they had not realized how much they must have exerted themselves till they settled for the night. They were now under the branches of some primrose trees. The trees had a delightful appearance compared to the common beech trees they had mostly seen since leaving the brambles. The only problem was that the primrose trees all seemed in competition with each other, trying to convince one and all which one was the most delightful. It was as if each tree was looking for constant affirmation that they were more charming than the other. This happened so much that their charm started to wear off. Their inherit delightful persons became contrived and manipulative, trying to force their charismatic status over one another.

Sam's newly discovered muscles, aching from all his hopping, preoccupied him, or this would have really bothered him. Mim was so self-consumed with his ever-constant jabbering that he successfully drowned out any pleas from the primrose about which tree was more alluring than the other. After a while, Sam and Mim could not go any longer and called it a night. Both drifted off to sleep, the primrose in Sam's dreams competing with the primrose in Mim's dreams.

Sam awoke and was thankful that the primrose had yet begun to welcome the new day with their narratives, and the vocal Mim was still fast asleep. "Awe, peace and quiet", thought Sam, but as often in life, once he had the peace and quiet to think, he wanted a break from doing the very thing he had desired previously. Thinking of what Gloria said about trusting one's scent seemed to hold some truth. Sam stretched his sore muscles he now knew he had, and took in a deep breath of the fragrant, warm violet blossoms of the primrose trees without them having to tell him which tree smelled best.

Suddenly, Sam was knocked to the ground in a flash. Sitting on top of him was a squirrel with a floppy straw hat, with a strange look in his eyes. Not that his eyes were strange, as much as they did not seem focused on anything in particular. "Howdy!" said the squirrel. At this moment, the squirrel jumped off to the side, fending wildly about him. Mim had awakened, and this was a squirrel. Mockingbirds, as mentioned, do not care for squirrels, and this squirrel had been on top of the only friend Mim ventured to have ever found that could endure him for more than a day. "Get away from me, dang blasted, you confounded jay birds," shouted the squirrel. "I am, not am, or was, a ja jaw jay, not today or any other da da day, not am, and you attacked my Sam!" scolded Mim defiantly, as he batted his wings against the bewildered squirrel. Sam got up and let out a loud bark, instantly stopping the shenanigans of Mim and the squirrel.

Sam might have been a small dog, but he was still a dog and bigger than those two put together. This loud outburst had awakened the primrose, and they then thought it was their chance to prove which one had enough charm to rectify the situation, taking credit for the armistice along with some compliments. Sam, in frustration, howled, and all became quiet. The primrose gave up trying to prove anything, except for one, which made a half-hearted plea of "but, you still think I'm pretty, right?"

"Who are you?" said Sam, addressing the squirrel. The squirrel, looking in Sam's direction, but not quite his direction, while keeping his arms protectively over himself in Mim's general direction, but not exactly his direction, said, "My name is Henry, brother, and what are ya doing keeping company with a bunch of blue jays?" "I ta tah told you, I am not a jay, and I am only one, not tatata two or three, you can clearly sa sa see na na nut hoarder!" said an offended Mim. "Well, I can't see how many you are, and you sure acted like a bunch of jays with all that rhetoric coming out of your bill," said Henry. Sam looked at the squirrel, which was kind of looking at Mim but not, and then at Mim. "Wait a minute, you really can't see? You mean you are blind?" questioned Sam. "What does blind mean, brother?" said Henry, taken aback. "Ba bah blind means you can't see, look, and na know what's to be, you can't sah see," exclaimed Mim with some vinegar in his tone. "I know well enough, and if you are not a jay, then you might be a crow with that scarf I felt around your neck. You crows are always taking things and hoarding them, more than all the nuts I might have foraged in my lifetime," said Henry, countering Mim. It then dawned on Sam that Henry was right. Not that Mim was a jay or a crow, and thankfully, there was not more than one Mim to put up with, but that Mim had a scarf around his neck.

As a matter of fact, it was a brilliant scarlet scarf. Sam had been so astonished by this new sense of seeing colors in this vibrant realm that the oddity of the brilliantly colored scarf on Mim was something he somehow had failed to notice before. While Sam had this revelation that Mim had a scarf and Henry was blind, the primrose felt cheated that all their attempts to show their beauty to this squirrel over the last couple of days had been for naught.

All stood silent, including the primrose trees. Then, there was a growling noise heard. It was not coming from Mim, Henry, or especially the primrose, who would have thought such a noise would have been totally against their ideal of beauty. It was coming from Sam, but not from his mouth. Sam just realized that since his arrival at this place, he had not eaten. Henry noticed the sound and said to Sam, "Are you hungry, brother?" Mim, not wanting to share and risk losing the only friend he ever thought he might find, said, "Here, ha ha here, have some of my lah linden berries. I mean, have some of our linden ba bah berries," as he hopped between Sam and Henry. Sam looked at the tiny berries and said with a wince, "I am not even sure those are really berries?" "Oh, they are ga gah great, with such a wonda wunda wonderful ta tah taste!" said Mim, trying to endorse them. Sam smelled them and stepped back, shaking his head in an affirmative "no."

"Well, what do you usually eat, brother?" said Henry. "Beef, pork, or these little bits that are bigger than those berries and smell a lot more appealing," said Sam, annoyed that they did not know what anyone ate. "What is beef?" said Henry. "What is pa pah pork?" said Mim. "Bits?" Said Henry and Mim, then, at the same time, looking at each other, disturbed that they both agreed on something they knew nothing about. "You know, cows, pigs, bits that come in a bag from the store," said Sam beside himself. "Ohhhh," said Henry softly. Sam's two companions then became very uncomfortable. "What is wrong? Can you two act normal, and tell me what I said that has made you two clam up like this?" demanded Sam. "I heard of cows and pigs, though never the bit people. They left a long time ago, along with the deer and others, and probably why Vovk's people then left because then they had nothing to eat," said Henry apprehensively, as if he just might have said too much.

Mim started going into a panic and was more hysterical than normal, which is a lot to believe. Finally, Mim was able to stutter out, "so it, it, tatatta, it's true. Vovk's people ate other pa pah… people." Sam looked at Mim and thought the bird was going to faint. "Wait, wait, wait," said Henry, "You are too small to be one of Vovk's people. Tell me, are you a youngin'?" said a pensive Henry. "I should say not!" said Sam with conviction. "Then you cannot be one of Vovk's people. Way too small. Way too small indeed. You must be more like a raccoon or a possum or something?" Sam proudly lifted his head and said, "I am a Scottish Terrier." "Well, da duh that settles it, we are safe!" said a relieved Mim, regaining his composure. "I have an idea. Stay right here. I won't be gone for long," said Henry, and with that scurried off the path.

After about an hour of Sam enduring Mim finding different ways to rhyme the phrase, "let's leave without him", Henry returned. With his face barely visible from the bounty he was carrying, Henry dropped a load of fruit in front of Sam. Before Sam was an apple and an assortment of berries, ranging from strawberries to blueberries. Sam tasted the blueberries and the strawberries with a less-than-approving response, but the apple didn't taste half bad. All things considered, in his hungry state, the apple tasted pretty dang good, and the berries could suffice. "Thank the Lord above you found me, brother, or you might have perished," said Henry. "He's not ca cah coming with us! I can find those without his ha ha helping you," said Mim jealously.

Sam smiled at Mim and said, "And how are you going to bring me the apple, or how many trips of berries do you think it will take till I have my fill?" Mim jumped up and down in a fit because Sam was right. "Un ba bah believable, traveling with a sca scah squirrel… with a va vah varmint. If my ma mah fellow mockingbirds witness da dah this, I will be sha sha shamed." shouted Mim hopelessly. "If it's any consolation, I won't be able to see you traveling with me and promise not to tell a soul," said Henry, smiling. Sam's pack then became three, and all three headed down the path together once Sam had eaten. "By the way, what's your name, brother?" said Henry. "My name is Sam, and that guy is named Mim," said Sam, much to Mim's chagrin. It seemed that not only is it possible for a blind squirrel to find nuts, but they can also find friends.

# Chapter 9

## STONE KEPT A FALLIN' GORGE

Stone People
Falling...
Gorge

# The Runt Oak

It was already evening, and there was still no word about the whereabouts of Sam. Ian was usually in his room, busy with one thing or another, but those things didn't matter now. A paradoxical desire: Ian wanted to talk, but also didn't want to speak with a soul. Sam's absence left Ian in limbo. His mom knew this state of being before and remembered when her mother had passed away. Vivian's mother was in critical condition after a heart attack. Throughout, Vivian repeatedly questioned the doctors after the procedure, desperately trying to restart her mother's heart. Though she kept getting the same vague responses from the doctors, Vivian kept asking the same questions as if maybe if she asked long enough, the answers would change and everything would be alright. Ian was now moping about downstairs, asking his mom the same repetitive questions about finding Sam to relieve his anxious mind while taking momentary pauses looking out the window for him, and then going back to his mom and repeating this trance of helplessness all over again. Vivian knew better than to turn him away and patiently followed the routine. It did not give answers, but it was an active method to oddly keep hope alive.

This cycle consumed Ian when Vivian approached him with a flashlight. Ian looked at his mom and, in frustration, said he had already checked the yard numerous times. The thought of walking around outside the house seemed pointless to him, though he was sure to do it again. Ian still took the flashlight from his mom's hand, since searching around the house really was just as productive, if not more, than asking questions.

Ian breathed heavily, and his mom stopped him. "I need your help in the kitchen." Ian followed his mom into the kitchen, and she led him to the sink. "I was washing dishes, and your grandmother's ring always slides off in the soap. The ring fell down the drain, and I cannot search and hold a flashlight," said Vivian, as she was looking down the sink, waiting for Ian to shine a light down the drain. Ian let out a groan, and after a moment of fidgeting about in protest, shown the light over Vivian's head.

Ian thought he was going to scream, and was trying his hardest to hold it back with what seemed a fruitless task. Sam was missing, and he was a party to something, which at the moment made no sense to him. Vivian could feel her son and said, while moving her head back and forth, looking down the drain, "Don't be like your father and stop thinking about only yourself." Ian mumbled something incoherent, which never really materialized because his mom had a point, and it reminded him that no matter how much resentment he had towards his father, there was a part of him, in him, he needed to learn from. "This isn't helping. The light only shows so much, and the sink seems to go on forever in the darkness," said an equally frustrated Vivian, who was then faring no better than Ian.

Sam, Mim, and their new companion Henry had been faring all right before they noticed an obstruction up ahead. As they came closer, the path stopped at what looked like a break in the road. The break appeared to be more than just that; it was a chasm, a fair distance separating the road from its continuation on the other side. Sam stopped before they had gotten any closer to see how far the chasm might go. "Mim, go on ahead and look down that crack in the road and tell us how deep it is," said Sam. Sam might have been able to garner enough courage to descend the stairs in his house, but that was just the stairs, and he knew where the floor would eventually end. Mim, in protest, started hopping around, and then looked at Sam as if to say, "Are you serious?" Sam looked at Mim, his fear of heights taken precedent, "and don't tell me we can just hop over this one!" Mim let out a screech, "Will not get ca cah close, will not hop and then pop, by cracky I will crack if I fa fah fall down that crack!" "Just fly over it and look silly, bird," said Henry. Mim let out a sigh and then burst out, "I cannot fa fah fly, nor can Sam or you, try and fly and I would da duh die!!!" Henry, bewildered, said, "Can't fly? I know you are a mockingbird, but aren't you taking this whole mocking business a little too far?"

Henry moved a little ahead of them and looked at what he could not see. While Mim and Henry had been debating, Sam noticed a sign to the right of the break in the road. Though Sam had not been able to speak human talk out loud, it had not stopped him from learning to read from all the books Ian had lying about his room. Sam read the sign out loud, "STONE KEPT A FALLIN' GORGE." "Da duh dat that is pa pah pretty far down, down to no ga gah ground," said Mim, turning to Sam. When Sam and Mim had stopped looking at each other, they turned to see Henry, who had gotten farther ahead, breaking into a run, running fast right towards the gorge!

Both Sam and Mim started shouting, "stop, stop, STOP!" But it was too late; Henry disappeared down the gap which barred their way. A distraught Sam screamed, "Didn't you ever learn how to read?" Mim, in disbelief, looked at Sam, "How, who, huh huh how could he la lah learn? He is ba bah blind." Sam, with a blank stare, looked towards the chasm, and Mim softly said, "He wa wah was blin…" unable to finish the word of Henry's apparent undoing.

Sam and Mim just stood there for what seemed an eternity. Both could not move forward. Fear prevented them from approaching closely enough to see the chasm's depth, and they also feared seeing far enough to witness Henry's gruesome fate. They turned from the chasm and started looking around, searching if there were any other options. This search did not last long, when all of a sudden, they heard Henry's voice. There was Henry on the other side of the chasm!

"It's f___ ju__go…" shouted Henry, with his voice fading in and out in the distance, beckoning Sam and Mim to come forward so they could see and hear. "It's fine, just go over to the edge and look," said Henry, as the two came forward and his words became more audible. Sam and Mim, with still a little hesitation, made their way to the edge of the chasm. "Look down already," said Henry, as the sun shone on him from the other side.

Sure enough, the daunting chasm was not that daunting at all. One could see the bottom and even make out a variety of details because it was only about three feet deep. "Well, I'd I'd a bah be hog swaggled," said Mim, hopping down the edge into the chasm. Sam scooted down the incline at the edge, and Henry tilted his head down on them. "Just follow the chasm to your left. It has a trail which leads up to the top of the other side. It curves up in no time, brothers."

The only part of the gorge floor, if you still wanted to call what amounted to a ditch, going by the grandiose name, which could now make the going difficult, was the amount of rocks past travelers must have thrown before to gauge the break from afar. While Mim blabbered along in his usual way, following the natural terrace leading up, Sam experienced the only real problem with the gorge. The chasm's breaking of the earth's crust had exposed various roots of the surrounding trees, and their woes made their issues even more apparent, being so close to them. Seemed all the trees were worried about issues that they were not even confident existed but yet petrified about, as they bickered among each other for comfort to the dismay of their discomfort.

# The Runt Oak

With so many voices expressing their presence at once, it was hard for Sam to even make out the gist of their complaints. What he could make out was a lot of 'them', 'they', and 'those people'. For a lot of references compromising the whole, it still came across as one of the most selfish, self-serving tirades he had ever heard. Sam was thankful when the side path led up to the other side, and just as thankful to leave the resounding conversations he had to endure below.

Henry greeted Sam and Mim. Henry came running to them and, unable to place them exactly, ended up hugging a birch tree, which wasn't too emotionally prepared for the sudden act of compassion. Sam nudged Henry to inform him of his miscalculation, and then stepped to the side, resulting in Henry giving Mim a hug. Mim squawked and skirted out of the hug. "Pa pah please you sah silly squirrel… wa wah wait! I am all sta stah sticky… and ba bah blue. What did you da dah do to me!" shouted Mim, trying to clean his feathers. Sam licked him, trying to help, and said, "Blueberries!"

Henry pointed to a pile of blueberries, which he had gathered when he had reached the other side. "Just keeping up my end of the bargain, but what is a giant Sa Sas… Sasquatch?" inquired Henry. "Can you say that again?" said Sam. "Giant Sasquatch?" replied Henry. Trembling, Sam (being familiar with the name from one of Ian's books about mythology) asked Henry why he wanted to know. "Well, that birch tree just told me he would tell me what I needed to know if I would only stop hugging him. Said it could be found a day's march from here," stated Henry. "Wa wah what's a su su succubus watch has to ta tah do with us?" said Mim, frightened. "He did not say succubus watch, but don't see how that makes it any better," said Sam, not feeling any more relieved. "Well, what is it, regardless of what cha wanna call it, brother?" pleaded Henry.

Sam acted as if he did not hear Henry. He knew one thing: if such an encounter was necessary, given the vague instructions to follow the path and get home, then it was unavoidable. Sam looked at his two companions, who were confused and disturbed by the words the birch tree had said. Sam turned to the birch trees and tried to remember which tree Henry had hugged. "They all look the same to me," said the blind squirrel. Sam groaned and approached the birch, but as soon as he got close, they all started saying, "We said nothing. Nope, not one thing. The Colonel can't blame us." All the birch then became silent and refused to say another word.

Sam went back to the middle of the path and joined his companions. "Well, brother, what did they say?" an anxious Henry asked. Sam looked at his two waiting eyes, which saw from within, looking for a response. Sam sighed, putting on a cheerful face, though they could hardly see it through his moustache, and his own eyes said something else. "They said to stay on the path is all, and that is exactly what we will do," said Sam. Sam's answer did not reassure them as Sam intended, but if they had to stay on the path, well, after all, he was their friend. Depending on his dog's sense of unwavering loyalty, how could they desert him?

Sam then laughed, and it was a sincere one that made everyone feel a lot better. "Wa wah so fa fah funny Sam?" said Mim. Sam, looking back at the backside of the sign, said, "There is writing on the other side of that sign, it says 'till it reaches the bottom, which is not far'." "Well, my pappy always said, there are two sides to every story", said Henry. Mim started to mumble some incoherent words, and then said, "a ah enough about this ba bah blasted sign. Let's get going and as far away from these succubi ba bah birch people as we ca cah can. Who knows who could be wa wah watching." As they started down the path, Henry turned to Mim, "I heard you when I started running towards that ditch. You care about me." Mim did not know what to say, but any words he could have said to dispute his feelings would not have mattered to Henry. Henry spent his whole life feeling more than seeing, and with Mim and Sam, he felt he belonged.

"Well, I'll be!" said Vivian, proud of herself, as she handed Ian a wrench she had been using. The pipe, which she unfastened below the sink, produced the ring they had been searching for. Seemed the darkness of the drain did not go on forever, but merely shifted in a curve which had blocked out their attempts to view the ring. After the curve, her grandmother's ring rested comfortably; no water had pushed it past the curved pipe's attachment point.

Ian managed a smile. Seeing his mom happy with her achievement made him momentarily forget about Sam. Vivian then took the flashlight from Ian's other hand and said reassuringly, "We need to save those batteries for when Sam shows up." As they walked into the kitchen, Ian's mom gave him a hug, saying, "I know you wanted to find my ring. I saw you smile." as she dried off the ring and slipped it back on her finger. Ian did not know what to say, being surprised before he had a chance to continue worrying about Sam again. Her son, though, did not have to respond- Vivian felt him.

# Chapter 10

## INTELLIGENCE PETRIFIED, WISDOM PERSONIFIED

# The Runt Oak

Since our valiant party had continued on, no one had said much. There was a feeling of apprehension in the air, and Sam had not dared to bring up the harrowing words of the birch trees again- or anything else, for that matter. Sam insisted on leading the way, and he kept his head down with his nose to the ground. One would have thought he was simply taking Gloria's words to trust his scent to heart, but in reality, this was not the case. Uneasy fear filled Sam's heart. Sam kept his head down, more trusting his eyes than his nose. After all, Sam did not know what a Bigfoot might smell like. Sam was looking out for footprints- big footprints. Sam wanted any heads up he could muster by keeping his head down. Ian's fascination for sculpting monsters from myth to mere clay did not leave out the reality of danger, which Sam was now wary of. Sam was being vigilant for Sasquatch- for Bigfoot.

"I have an erratic bird that refuses to fly. I have a blind squirrel that will run through a wall for me, or rather a chasm, and I have a responsibility I have never asked for," thought Sam, as he tried to multitask the burdens in his mind. This also made Sam think of Ian, Vivian, and his Uncle Jake, who all shouldered their own weight of responsibilities, since Greg had left them his weight to carry. Sam thought of the simple responsibilities which did not seem so simple anymore, as his people feeding him every day, or taking him to the vet (which he never realized they despised as much as him). Sam felt the weight of multiple worlds on his shoulders. This strange world made the weight even heavier. The unknown hides our greatest fears. A world he seemed entrusted to save… a world that constantly discouraged him.

# Intelligence Petrified, Wisdom Personified

Sam wondered what the heroes in all the movies he and Ian watched would do. Sam wished he was with Ian now, watching them figure it out from the comfort and safety of a couch. Then there were the trees, which appeared to be the root of this world's problems. Keeping his head so low also made the constant friction of the trees and their issues even more resounding. Vibrating words rising from under the ground clouded Sam's mind, which was now under siege from all directions.

Eventually, it became easier for Sam to survey the path for the dreaded footprints. Not because he found some newfound courage, or revelations to solve the dilemma, but because the ground which might allude to an ominous presence was becoming increasingly less to study. Sam had not noticed it at first, but when the proximity of the trees and their words of conflict became closer, he realized it was because the path was becoming narrower, which drew the trees near. The three companions were now getting up close and personal with some beech trees which lined the path, and all the personal comments from the beech people seemed less than sincere.

Again, the appearances did not match the truth. Nobody was really doing fine. None of these trees was doing as great as they wanted others to believe. The trees' current deceptive state of mind made Sam's refusal to expand on the questions of Bigfoot to Mim and Henry no different than the avoidant nature of the trees. This realization was the worst part of it all for Sam- lack of communication and the sincerity that gave it meaning. As all this was building along the confines of the narrowing path when the path opened up through the dark foliage, and the three were suddenly basking in full sunlight and open air.

The beech trees were behind them, and in front of them was an empty hill which stretched a fair distance towards a high point surrounded by mist. Refusing to go back, they took the path which was still before them. As this entered this desolate surrounding, there was a quiet that enveloped them. Looking now at what seemed at first jagged rocks, now resembled trees- white and grey. This barren, yet occupied, landscape of half-fallen trees littered the path all around them. Henry was the first to notice the path had become very hard. The path seemed almost as if carved out of rock, and he could hear Mim's feet clearly hopping on the path and their echo replaying in the silence.

After recovering from the awe of this vast change in scenery, Sam returned his attention to the ground. "What is that? What is…" said Sam as his gaze froze on what he saw on the path floor- footprints! There were footprints, sure enough, but not large ones. Paw prints, claw prints, and an assortment of various creatures that had left their mark before engraved the path. Sam smelled one print, and they definitely were not fresh. Henry felt one of them, and the tracks were definitely not recent. Mim then spoke up, "They are ca cah carvings?" "No, they are fossils," said Sam with a sigh of relief and awe. "What wa wha are fa fah fossils?" said Mim. "They are hardened relics of past life… way past life," said Sam. "I have seen them in books about dinosaurs." Sam then understood this whole hill was like an ancient grave, all embedded in petrified wood and past life.

"Sort of feels like a mass grave. I mean, one would think a graveyard this size would be a lot creepier, my brothers," said Henry. "Well, it takes thousands of thousands of years for this to happen," said Sam in a scholarly tone. "Well, wa wha whatever they da duh were, they wha were, were way ba bah back… and huh huh how this happened was wha way back… ruh right?" said an unsure Mim. Sam nodded in agreement and did not even want to entertain other possibilities. "Let's get 'er going, because I do not want to stay long enough to become stone and find out," said Henry, and he started following the path up the broad hill. There was, though, an inclination on Sam's part that wished Henry would slow down just a little. Sam welcomed the peace; the petrified roots of these trees had little to say. Getting closer to the summit, they noticed rustic colors again fading in and out of the mist. These colors then took shape, the shape of imposing architecture.

This was nothing like his house and the hallway upstairs that Sam saw at floor level- that perspective at home where his imagination suggested columns and pediments. These columns were gigantic, imposing a visual that his imagination could have never reached. Reaching the top of the hill, something else became even more astounding. What was currently before them was not some temple of the gods, an ancient city from antiquity, not even architecture… but the trunks of colossal trees.

As they walked into this grove of giants, one would have thought this imposing presence, that seemed to go upwards with no end, would cause them to be nervous, but it did not. Actually, it had the opposite effect. The barren hill of petrified trees gave peace, lacking the bombardment of conflicting thoughts. The grandeur of these trees gave not only peace but comfort. Most amazing were the thoughts and feelings of these giants. Their minds, and even their hearts, were present, and they were void of stress. At first, it was hard to make out their words, but only to feel their solace. Their voices were low, like waves on the ocean. Then, once Sam and his companions had adjusted to the calmness, they slowed down in time with the voices. This is what the voices said:

"Welcome, be at peace seekers. Such a blessing to count three, for the seeker is usually alone. The seeker thinks inward and not outward. You have found similar hearts to filter the antics of the mind. Others, not the seekers themselves, contrive the mind's motives. Please do not stand on our doorstep. Come inside and bring you with you. You are accepted by us. We desire you. We value you, you and you."

# The Runt Oak

Sam, Mim, and Henry walked forward, and they felt good. They felt good about being who they were. Sam and Henry hardly recognized Mim, who became content being quiet with himself. They passed the enormous trunks, which lined the path at a respective distance. The mist which surrounded the exterior through which they entered cleared, and they could look upwards as they approached a clearing that let in the sun. Thirteen trees marked the clearing, all forming a perfect circle around the open space. "Come forward, seekers, so we may see you. Seek the sunlight and our hospitality", said a low, fatherly voice.

They walked into the middle of the circle. Standing there looking up, they saw the trunks of the large trees go ever upward and into the clouds above. Then, they heard many voices in a low melodic rumble. They were speaking in harmonies, each with different thoughts, and yet in unified acceptance with one another. Sam felt as if he was being hugged by Ian. Mim felt the security of his nest when he was young. Henry felt tears of happiness run down his eyes, eyes that could not see but were feeling much more. Then the three companions heard their names, felt their names, and felt safe. After this feeling of security had its gentle say, they heard thirteen voices speak.

"My name is Antonius. My name is Anthony. My name is Anthony, but no more or no less. My name is Thaddeus. My name is Noah. My name is Hector."

Then a moment of silence fell. The fragrant scent, reminiscent of gentle April rain, now filled the air. The low voices continued, but in a more nurturing tone…

"My name is Olga. My name is Helen. My name is Olena. My name is Olena, but no more or no less. My name is Ada. My name is Silvia."

# Intelligence Petrified, Wisdom Personified

There was a moment of silence. There was another moment of silence. Then there was a laughter among the voices, which was broken by a cheerful, even deeper voice which had first addressed them. "Oh, it is my turn," said the deeper voice, and there was another roll of soothing laughter among the prior voices. "Wanted to be sure all my brothers and sisters had their moment in the sun to be appreciated for who they are. My name is Anton, and our names are defined by what we do. We again welcome you, seekers."

Overcome by joy, Henry was the first to respond, "Brothers!" They could feel smiles all around them as Mim finally said something, "sa sasa sisters too!" Sam did not know what to say and said, "Brothers and sisters, you sure are big." Laughter erupted throughout the grove and seemed to resonate in the sky above. The deep voice of Anton answered in a solemn tone, "We are Sequoyah." "Just as the birch told us, we found you brothers… and sisters!" said Henry with excitement. "But you said Sasquatch among those birch trees?" said a confused Sam. "Yes, that's it. I remember clearly now. Sequoyah, Sasquatch, I was close enough. That birch was not exactly forthcoming when he whispered that to me," reflected Henry nonchalantly.

Sam was about to let Henry know how much that 'close enough' had rattled him, but felt it best to let sleeping dogs lie- though he couldn't get any rest when he was looking behind every tree for a Bigfoot. Anton then laughed heartily at Sam. "Sam, you should tell him. I think he would like to know. Know how it made you feel. Know what a Sasquatch is… a big FOOT!" said Anton, putting a good-natured emphasis on the end of 'foot'.

Henry looked at Sam inquiringly. "Well, Henry, a Sasquatch is a gigantic creature. Some say it is a monster. It is a big creature with big feet," said Sam, trying not to sound angry. "Big feet, big feet," laughed the Sequoyah trees, and Sam felt a gentle nudge on his hind leg as Mim hopped up in the air. The tip of a massive root had popped up from the ground and was making itself known. "Oh, stop that, Anthony," said a deep but sweet voice. "But that was not me, Olena," roared a jovial, deep voice. "Not you, the other Anthony," giggled Olena, sounding like a gurgling brook. The other Anthony removed the root from under Sam and Mim and said, "Just letting you know that your use of big can be rather small around here." Henry looked in the direction of Sam and hesitantly said, "Did a Bigfoot just show up?" Sam chuckled, "No, it was no Sasquatch but a Sequoya. I forgive you, and it was my fault for not telling you what one was. If I did, you might have then told me you were not sure what the birch said… knowing the severity of the word."

"But Sam, tell him about Sequoya?" bellowed Anton. "It's a tree, a big redwood tree," said Sam, answering Anton. "No, Sam, tell him all about Sequoya," said Anton, as all the other trees made a low hum as in reverence. "I don't understand?" said Sam meekly. "Then I will tell you, son of Vovk," said Anton. The leaves about them rustled as if settling down for a comfortable listen, and Anton resumed.

"Sequoya was a Cherokee, a native people of Sam's world. They knew of trees, the difference in trees, all of nature, including Vovk's people. When others came to subdue them, these strangers took from the Cherokee. They took their land as if it were theirs to take, but this was not enough. Sequoya's people were pressured by them to adopt their dress, worship, and language. They, in essence, wanted the Cherokee to no longer be Cherokee but one of a whole. They wanted the Cherokee to be 'people' but only the same as all people. Many Natives named themselves 'the people', but the keyword is 'the' people, their people. Language is an important part of who people are. Our language is how we shape our thoughts. It is how we offer our unique contribution to our world. The Natives never wrote their language in symbols, so the strangers thought it would be easy to eradicate this part of their being, making them people but not the people. So, Sequoya put his people's language into symbols. He made it possible for one to see and hear what they wanted to say in their original voice. The individual is important. The individual is important to me."

There was then a low vibration of approval from the other trees in the circle. Sam and his companions heard thirteen voices approve, all in their individual voices. "It is good to be named after Sequoya. There is a meaning which says I am."

"Yes, I remember him now. He was in one of Ian's books. He had a turban on his head, just like Sinbad. But how do you know about the Cherokee?" asked Sam.

"Sinbad is one I do not know, and thank you for bringing him to our attention. One can never know everything, and not knowing is an opportunity to become wiser. Oh, we know of the Cherokee people. These profound thoughts permeate and transcend a single world. In the annotation of our thoughts, we keep the spelling of him and us as 'Sequoya' and not 'sequoia' in a brotherhood of shared existence," stated Anton in a dignified voice.

"Our roots run deep."

# Chapter 11

# KEEPING UP APPEARANCES

# The Runt Oak

There was no friction of voices, but there was also no peace, unlike the petrified hill. It was a dark hollow, far from the current location of our seekers and the Sequoyah. All about was pitch-black, except for a disheveled-looking tree house perched on top of a dying tree. The only sign of life was the life leaving. An insect made its way up the trunk of the tree to join a few others, going nowhere in particular. The insects appeared busy, but they really had no purpose. Maybe they were waiting for something to die so they could partake in the aftermath of life- the scavengers of the contents of a coffin. If this was the case, they would be severely disappointed, for this cycle of death was never-ending in the dark recesses of where they were. If one would have been one of these insects, you would have finally heard some voices within if you had ventured close enough to the decaying house.

This house was boarded up as if to hide from those outside. The tree house seemed wedged, even forced, between branches where it never really belonged. If one was, then one of these insects, and if one would have had the courage to venture inside, this is something they would eventually realize- this house was like the truth turned inside out, it was constructed to lie, acting like an institution of enlightenment. Oh, the lights were on inside the house, but certainly nothing enlightening.

In retrospective, light seems to be an ironic word to use, because the interior of this place was lit with artificial light. The genuine light, the natural light of truth, was never let in. Rotten wood planks, reapplied too many times to count, formed the exterior. The addition of each plank made its intended purpose less successful—just as each lie meant to cover another lie becomes less convincing. The foundation of this place had eroded a long time ago, but inside, its inhabitants still refused to accept the truth.

In all truth, there was a little insect that had made its way in. It's only proper that we infringe on this toxic space with at least a little of truth, so one can get a nonobjective look through the manipulation within. This bug was one of the smaller entities, which always latches onto such fake personas, desperately looking to feel relevant. Guilt by association, contrived to be important by association. Unlike the debilitated exterior, the interior was as lavish as any mansion.

This determined disciple made its way across a richly adorned rug, under some ornate furniture, to a mahogany desk, which sat the conceited ruler of this fabricated domain. The insect then waited on the master of the house, spending its time impressed by the magnificence of the accumulated knick-knacks which served as a substitute for security. The owner paid little attention to the insect and hardly even noticed it was there. It was an owl preoccupied, talking to his guest. The insect could have been a bear, and the owl's self-ego would still have probably not have noticed him. The self-absorbed owl continued to talk in a high, affluent manner to a stately-dressed raccoon, which was seated in a leather chair.

The owl, with an omnipotent stare at his masked visitor, carried on, "And can you believe, after all I offered, all my valuable advice, they just ignored my suggestions? The nerve of them after all I have done for everyone. Let me tell you, I know a thing or two, Cyrus about dams… which would fix all the problems them simpletons are having down by the river bottom. I remember how my great-great-great uncle's involvement, and his involvement alone, prevented the great flood those many springs days ago. I, coming from such an illustrious family, and being a colonel on top of that, and those peons hardly ever taking the time and know-how to sacrifice so much for so little, as my family and I have done since time immemorial. You are fortunate to have me as a friend; it is only my humility which prevents me from making this whole realm acknowledge my significance for the sake of history."

The raccoon, dazed by another of the Colonel's long-winded lectures, came to long enough to catch a gist of the owl's current drama. "I remember the epic tales of that event well, but don't see how a dam now can prevent the current erosion, especially since that river bottom is all dried up. Nonetheless, the actions of your greatest uncle are legendary… well, if not biblical, from what you tell me," said Cyrus.

The Colonel, as usual, when one was critical of his opinion, changed the subject, as if all Cyrus just said held no relevancy. "That is a really nice waistcoat you have on, Cyrus. Granted, it's not as splendid as the one my great, greater, greatest uncle passed down to me, but still not too bad. If you lost a few pounds, it would fit better. I was lucky to be born with an impressive figure and have no issues with formal wear. I was a striking image in uniform," stated the proud owl.

Then suddenly, the house shuddered, and everything shook. Cyrus grabbed an urn which was falling off an end table, and the Colonel watched one of his lamps fall while he flew up to the safety of a chandelier that swung above. "Stop being so useless, Cyrus! why did you not catch that lamp while I was saving the chandelier?" said the owl, becoming angry. Cyrus timidly put down the urn, which was heavy enough, trying to balance what remained of the lamp back to an upright position.

This happened often to the unstable house every time an unexpected gust of wind (much like the owl's mood swings) came along. Putting all the belongings back in place, the Colonel directed Cyrus' attention to a photo that had slid off his mantle. "See? As I was saying, what a fine figure of a bird I was in uniform," said the Colonel, admiring himself. "Isn't that a captain's insignia on your jacket?" said Cyrus, studying the photo. The Colonel then gave the raccoon an uneasy look. "It's an old photo and does not give a clear image of the uniform. I surely was a colonel, and I advise you not to insult my service in the future. It was only because of my extreme humility that I declined a generalship. Who needs all that hassle? When I could still handle and accomplish everything asked of me beyond all expectations, on a par with a higher rank. I dread the day they will probably want to put up a statue of me. I will have to deal with the jealousy of those which held a higher rank, but held less importance," boasted the owl. It should now be noted that it is no coincidence that arrogance and ignorance sound similar.

Turning back to his desk, the Colonel finally noticed the little insect which wanted to talk to him. The owl rotated his head towards the insect and listened to what it had to say. After a while, the Colonel drew back and went in a rage. "Who do they think they are?" shouted the owl. Suddenly, a book slammed down on the poor messenger, and the insect was no more. A shocked Cyrus said, "Man, what did you do that for?" "No bother about him. They are all the same, and there are plenty of them to take his place," and with that, the Colonel ate what remained of the bug.

After the owl had devoured the poor insect, he turned to the raccoon, "That stranger, and most of all those high and mighty 'sequoia' people! One thing I cannot stand is people sticking their noses in places they don't belong. Just dandy, an outsider with two local freaks talking to a bunch of old fuddy-duddies about our well-being. What do they know and what should they have the privilege to know? This is how it all starts, Cyrus. You allow a few 'different' people to ask questions of those who have no clue how the world works, and the next thing you know, everything becomes broken. You have a bunch of people with no direction, trying to rock a then-sinking boat. That is how societies with proper law and order end up at the bottom of the sea… by accommodating peculiar behavior, it has no room for. One must have control! Will definitely take it upon myself to make sure nothing goes awry… if I can find the time. What would this realm do without people like me addressing the weeds in the field? Thank goodness my kind is nocturnal, and I have such a vast library of such rare books. There will be no flying around tonight. I must use my time wisely and confirm my suspicions and solutions," said the Colonel, now perched proverbially on his high horse.

"Be careful, Colonel, you might get a nosebleed so high up there," said Cyrus. "What?" said the Colonel, too preoccupied hearing his own voice. "Nothing, Colonel, was just concerned about your sanity, I mean sah... safety (stuttered Cyrus backtracking). But I am curious, have you ever gotten around to actually reading all those books?" said the raccoon, already familiar with their individual placement, which never seemed to move on the shelves - one area he had often focused on when ignoring the Colonel's talk over the years.

"Reading them is just a ceremonial act for those who cannot understand. I said I might want to confirm my suspicions and solutions, not find them. What made me a great general was that I was not only practical but efficient. There is nothing in those books that I don't already know. Plus, reading them would just become more work, an obligation by wanting to report all their mistakes," said the Colonel with a grandiose sense of purpose.

Cyrus got up to leave, and the Colonel suddenly became somber, asking him where he was going. "It's late, just going home, and as always, I appreciate your intellect and delightful conversation, my friend," said Cyrus in false admiration, wanting to avoid any more of the owl's mood swings. "Yes, yes, of course, Cyrus. I believe you will be rather impressed when I tell you my observations later," said the Colonel, seeking more admiration. "There is only one, and you are the Colonel," said Cyrus, and as he opened the fancy front door on his way out, it caused another plank to come undone outside. Cyrus looked into the darkness and scampered down the tree, but stopped momentarily, catching sight of a few insects. Cyrus looked at them and sympathetically said, "Be careful, seems our modest Colonel might be a general now."

# Chapter 12

# THE WHISPERING PINES

# The Runt Oak

Ian bent down as he went under one of the hackberry trees, which crowded next to the opposite side of his backyard fence. No wonder the yard had an epidemic of hackberries; the source of the affliction populated the whole empty lot which bordered their house. Besides the hackberries, grass spurs infested the lot. Ian stopped and grabbed a stick, and started wiping them off his shoes, which had become loaded with them. This act reminded him of the one time his father confronted him about taking them off. "Boy, what the hell are you doing? No son of mine is going to take off them stickers like some pansy. Do it with your hands for God's sake?" Ian could still remember dropping the stick and feeling the points sink into his skin as he pulled the grass spurs out by hand. God had had no stake in the bloody business since some of the grass spurs were of the 'devil head' variety- the dark ones that had an ominous resemblance to a horned face from which they got their nickname.

This time, Ian had no intention of using his hands on these demonic looking burrs. Greg was not there, and neither would be the blood on his fingers for doing what he was told that day. After wiping off his shoes, Ian looked up and called out for Sam. Uncle Jake had told him a story about a dog which once got lost in the backwoods, and this large plot of land in back of his house sure qualified. Ian called and whistled, but there was no sign of Sam.

Ian trudged along through the underbrush till he reached the end of the lot, which was separated by a barbed wire fence. Debris, ranging from leaves and branches to man-made trash, covered the lower part of the fence.

# The Whispering Pines

This was not always the case, but since some land developers had set up a buffer farther up the road, the water washed down everything not nailed down onto this fence. The developers even had received some award for adverting flooding in their new housing district. Rumor also had it that some son of one developer who came up with the plan was going to have his statue put up as a testament to "working with nature and not against it". Well, there was a lot against it now, and it was all piled at the base of the fence. There was no way a little dog like Sam would have been able to get through this. If that was not enough, his shaggy fur would have certainly gotten hung up in all the undergrowth Ian just had to soldier through.

Ian looked over the fence at the pine trees, which thickly covered the opposite side. "Sam! Come on, boy… Sam!" but there was no Sam. Before Ian turned to walk back to his house, he gave out one last sharp whistle. Still, there was no Sam, but Ian could still feel him. Sam had to be alive. Ian knew he was alive… but where?

Sam and his friends, standing on the misty edge of the redwood grove, said their goodbyes to the Sequoyah. As usual, the Sequoyah answered back in their own individual voices while still finding harmony with one another. When Sam referred to them as a people, Anton the elder corrected him. Anton proposed that, if the word must be used, they should call themselves their own people, and acknowledge and accept others. Sam then thought it best not to even bother calling them by this extended version of 'people'. Sam felt relieved at not having to adhere to an identification, which never made sense to him to begin with.

"Never forget who you are, young seekers. You must be you to offer anything useful. Without being yourself, how can you be sincere? One can never reach an accord with another without trust. I am not saying to be selfish, but to react as yourself, taking into consideration the differences of another and how they might help you see even more. Only you do not comprise the world, for good reason. You are only part of the question and not the sum of the answer to what is true," said Anton to Sam. And Anton then turned his thoughts towards Henry and Mim, "and you to feel within young squirrel, and you to see and feel more within… and talk less young bird."

There was much affectionate laughter at Anton and his advice to Mim by the other Sequoyah. The Sequoyah got to know Mim very well by all he had to say, despite all he would often say. They got to know Henry by how often he felt their bark to know where they were. Last, they got to know Sam by how much he missed Ian, and what he missed revealed Ian too. What did the three seekers learn about the Sequoyah? They learned about themselves because the Sequoyah were superb listeners.

The companions felt a renewed vigor, a belief in who they were. This inner belief is what they needed most for what was to come. In most stories about the hero's journey, someone gives the hero a magic sword or shield. The Sequoyah gave them the magic within to wield the most powerful weapon and uphold the strongest defense a hero can have- confidence in who they are. In parting, the Sequoyah gave them their ultimate message. They saved the most important message for last. Sam and his companions, unlike the ancient trees, lacked the patience; time did not allow them to hear what centuries of experience could teach.

"Follow the path back down on the other side of our hill and follow it onward. You will eventually arrive at a tall forest. There you will find what one could say are our wayward little brothers, distant relatives, but be wary. Beware, for they were not strong and have fallen into disarray. Be vigilant of their whispers, but try to understand them. We have listened to you, and for you to succeed in your quest, you will now have to listen to yourself. Only this will save you, them, and all in this realm," then Anton was silent, but they could then feel his smile and those of his brothers and sisters who gathered around them.

As they crossed the threshold back onto the sloping hill of petrified wood, they heard the name Bohdan rise on the wind, which blew across the barren space in a melancholy crescendo from the female Sequoyah. The three were already sad to leave the compassionate counsel of the Sequoyah, and this strange last word made this sadness deeper, but also in some unexpected way gave hope.

It was much easier going down the petrified path than it had been going up. The caution was not going down too fast on the hard surface, which paved their way. The assorted indentions of the fossils also had to be traversed without tripping since they were larger here. Here on this side were the remains of fish, and the fish were much larger than the birds and animals which littered the ground on the opposite side. At one time, this was where water met land's edge, and all the assorted life from the depths of a mysterious ocean found their last resting place.

Before reaching the grass and trees at the bottom of the path, the companions passed a large fossil parallel to the entry to the hill. On closer inspection, Sam noticed it had been a whale. After finding their way around the physical eulogy of this once larger-than-life mammal, they looked back at the summit of the hill and the mist clouding it from afar. This made Sam think of the mist which must have shot up from the whale during its life, and he paused in reflection. Unlike the Sequoyah, the size of this whale did not protect it from its fate. If they were to survive this journey and be of any help to this world, it would come from the amount of belief they had in themselves and not their physical stature.

# The Runt Oak

As they entered the forest on this side, the path led them through a grove of sycamore trees. The chalice-like frames of the sycamores lined the path, and their branches were like fingers of a hand extending to their leaves on top. What was strange about the sycamores was that, unlike most other trees, their thoughts and words were unclear, yet they conveyed intense caution and paranoia. There was only a slight breeze, yet the leaves of the sycamore people shuddered and rustled constantly. It was as if they were having a nervous breakdown and could find no words. From time to time, the party believed they could distinguish a word or two, only to be met with silence. After this din in thought, the leaves would tremble more as if the trees thought they had said too much.

They finally were making it through the last remaining sycamores when they saw what lay up ahead. It was the base of what appeared to be more mountainous terrain, and on this slope were pine trees, so many pine trees that the path ahead was hard to make out. The wind then seemed to pick up, as Sam and Mim heard it hiss through the trees. Henry, who had to live his life relying on sound, heard something else and felt something else. Henry felt no wind, and heard no wind in the pine needles… Henry heard whispers, so many whispers.

Henry walked slowly towards the pines, which encompassed the view of the others. Getting closer, he veered from the path, and then back on the path, till he turned under the first boughs of a pine and shouted, "Someone, please help me, I don't know where I am!" Sam and Mim rushed towards the frightened squirrel. Sam took Henry's trembling hand, and Henry grabbed onto Sam's fur. "Mim, stop your chattering. And stop doing it in whispers. This is no time for a practical joke," said Sam, leading Henry back to the path which was infringed upon by the pines. When Sam did not hear Mim's expected chain of rebuttal, he saw the poor bird rolling on the path. "What in the world is a matter with everyone?" said Sam. Mim then started pleading, "it is not my muh muh fault. They threw me out of the tree. Mama, Papa, I am sa sah sorry. No, I did not fall out to be ba bah bad. Stop saying that… no; they did not pa pah push me out because I was different. I am sorry, so sorry, so so so sah sorry," as Mim then burst into tears.

Sam, with Henry holding onto his fur, went to calm Mim down. As he approached Mim, he tried to comfort him and heard the whispers, which were clearly not coming from Mim, say, "You are a runt, nobody wanted you. It is your fault that Ian is always alone… so needy, so needy. Your actions are incredibly selfish. You are a liability, you runt. You will doom all your friends. Friends? You have no friends, you have only pity. Such a runt-such an abomination towards Vovk's people."

The three companions huddled together under the pines, holding each other tight as they endured what seemed to be an interrogation. The whispers were unbearable and such nasty, hateful accusations. They even heard what appeared to be gossip, hurtful judgment about the lives of sycamores. A shrill whistle broke through the pines, pulling them from a bad dream. The whispers became quiet. Sam knew that whistle. It was Ian's call! "Come on, boy… Sam!" It was Ian's voice and not a whisper. Building in force, as it ushered out of the path which led inward into the pines. Sam and Mim heard it too. "Who is that?" said Henry. "It is my Ian, but where is he?" said Sam, no longer concerned with all the ugly words the whispers had been saying. "You're eh eh Ian, what being is a eh Ian?" asked Mim. "He is my friend, my Ian, and if he is somewhere in there… I am going to go in there and find him," said a resolute Sam.

# Chapter 13

## REBELS IN RED

# The Runt Oak

S am went into the dark pines, and as good friends Mim and Henry followed in trust. Words seemed to usher again from the dark spaces found within and around the large gatherings of pines. The companions closed ranks, and Sam turned to Henry, taking the necessary precautions. "I think it best you hold on to my fur again to be safe."

As Henry took hold of Sam to help guide him, the whispers that haunted them initially were taking shape again. Sam then turned to Mim, "if there ever was a time I would welcome your constant chattering, the moment is now." "Wa wha what do you want ma mah me to ta tah talk about?" answered Mim. "Something, everything, because right now anything is better than these seedy whispers which are reminding me about the time I was a pup and got in trouble for peeing on the rug!" implored Sam of Mim. "Yes, please, Mim," begged Henry, as he argued with some unseen antagonist about not being lazy, "no, no, no, I was prudent and did store enough nuts for the winter. I was not idle, I tell you. I couldn't see… how was I to know there was another hole at the bottom of the trunk where all my forage for the winter would fall out!" said the exasperated squirrel.

Mim was at a loss for words, but finally the mockingbird started his own mocking over the ever-increasing taunts, when the whispers implied they wanted to start a conversation about how turkeys could fly better than him. "You dah don't, na nah never had, real la leaves. Just na nah needles, like a bunch of old ga gah grandmother's ma mah making bah blankets," erupted Mim. At first, this snap back from the bird caught the whispers by surprise, till all the mocking on their personal character made them even more resentful than before.

Though Mim could be more than irritable, not letting in a word edge-wise, the barrage of insidious whispers from the pines started getting the upper hand. Everything got to a point that nobody could even think straight, not even the whispering pines. "Unlike others of Vovk's people, you cannot even fly the short distance which could get you to the bottom of the stairs," one whisper directed at Sam. Sam blinked his eyes in a befuddled manner. "That makes little sense. Dogs can't fly?" thought Sam to himself. "What do you know about anything, bird?" said another whisper toward Mim. "You are blind." At this, Henry, who was standing close by, said he was no bird, catching the taunt made for Mim. "Ma mah mealy heads, your ba bah blunt needles do not have that sha sha sharp inta intah intellect… da duh do you?" said a defensive Mim, rather pleased but also rather confused with himself.

Everyone realized that this unfair and disrespectful game targeted everyone. "You pathetic, spineless spruce of a pine, you are dampening our essence of freshness. You smell like elderberries," said one pine to another. The path along the pines became one chaotic barrage of unbearable nonsense. This jabber coming out of every nook and cranny was too much for even Mim to counter, and he even insulted himself, "the only ra rah reason you wa wha won't fly is bah because you are ska skah scared of pa people seeing how off your fah feather strips are on your wa wah wings are all crooked." Henry then said smugly, "I will have to remember that one the next time you open your mouth and wings, attempting to make fun of my hat, you silly bird."

Sam could not take any more and wished Ian was there. Remembering he could now whistle, Sam let loose a loud whistle, and all became quiet. Henry and Mim stopped their bickering and turned to see where the sound came from. Sam's companions were not the only ones that became quiet; it seemed the shrilled whistle silenced the pines too.

# The Runt Oak

They were all relieved by the sudden reprieve of accusations, but in the silence, it made Sam think of Ian and miss him more. Seeing an opportunity, the pines latched on to Sam's distraught state of missing Ian and attacked his emotional weak spot with more words of implied selfishness. "Whistle all you want, but they are only words in the wind, you selfish maggot. Ian deserted you, and these so-called friends here will desert you too,' said the hurtful whispers. Sam would not accept this and tried to call for Ian again, letting out an even sharper whistle. Again, all became silent. As if picking on Sam did not have the desired effect, the pines went after Henry, "Would not matter if you left that miniature wolf or not, you daffy squirrel. Would it really matter? You could not see if he was there or not, you blind acorn,' scoffed one whisper.

Then Mim whistled, and he jumped around with satisfaction as if he'd just had an epiphany. "Why are you so happy in this dreadful place? You might not realize that you can fly, but whistling is no big feat for a bird," said Sam, irritated. In a burst of cackling laughter, Mim said, "na nah no Sam. Da dah don't you see, huh, hear? They da dah don't like whistles," and Mim smiled. "The bird is right!" exclaimed Henry, and then had a peculiar look on his face, realizing he just said Mim was right about something.

It was true; it seemed sharp whistles made the whispering pines cease to whisper. The friends with this newfound knowledge followed the path, whistling in turn. It took Henry his share of tries, but when he had placed his paw in his mouth to feel why he could not whistle, he found placing his paw inside just right made his whistle even more resounding than his friends. So, they followed the path, letting out whistles. This continued for some time as they journeyed down the path through the vast forest of pines. Sam would whistle, then Mim, and then Henry.

After a while, they lost track of whose turn it was till they noticed why. It seemed they were not the only ones whistling.

Echoing about them, they heard other whistles. These were sharp and clear whistles that had depth to them, far more than either of them could muster. They were crisp and clear, almost metallic, like a hammer striking silver, and they were getting ever closer to them. "Could it be Ian?" thought Sam to himself. Sam started to run towards the ting of the whistles, and his companions ran and hopped to keep up with him.

As they ran forward some distance with no sign of Ian, Sam stopped, exhausted by the pace his adrenaline had taken them. During this interval which Sam had taken a breather, the pines had taken up their assault on the companions' sanity anew. Having no other recourse, they resumed walking to the cadence of their own whistles to thwart the pines. The whistles which had beckoned them forward before also started again. Sam noticed brief flashes of bright red among the pines, as these crisp, clear whistles seemed to be all around them. "What are all these figments of red popping in and out of the trees?" said Sam, as he looked into the pines. "Ma mah maybe they are cha cha cherries? I sure ca cah could use something to eat," said Mim. "Ouch!" then cried Henry, as he started hopping on one foot. "Just because I am huh huh hungry, you da dah don't have to make fa fa funny of me hu Henry," retorted Mim. "I am not making fun of you!" said Henry as he grabbed his foot in pain.

Looking down, Sam noticed Henry had stepped on a pine cone. "Stand still, Henry, let me look at your foot," said Sam. Sam went over to Henry and found the culprit. Not only had Henry stepped on a pinecone, but a pine needle still lodged in the cone had also pierced Henry's paw. "That tickles," said Henry as Sam licked the squirrel's foot to abstract the needle. "There!" Sam said after removing the pine needle from Henry. Just as Henry made a sigh of relief, they heard a voice yell, "Stop!" "What did we do?" shouted Sam at the unknown demand. Out of the pines came a red form which darted onto the path and knocked Mim over, who was currently doing something with the pinecone that Henry had cast aside after he had stepped on it.

Sitting on top of Mim was a red bird, a cardinal, to be exact. The whole path then became littered with the color red, as a whole slew of cardinals flew down. "Don't eat them!" said the cardinal, which rested on Mim. Out of the pinecone, Sam could then see insects pouring out. "Use them for shallow vanity, but don't take them within. They will make your mind and heart sick," said the Cardinal, as it crushed some bugs and rubbed them on his plumage, which caused its feathers to dazzle. Another cardinal bent its head down, looking at some of the bugs scurrying away off the path. "They are the problem. They cause the pines to whisper their hateful rhetoric. Down with the Colonel and his manipulative ways!" shouted the Cardinal with his crest on his head becoming fully erect.

All the cardinals then started chirping in their metallic voices, morphing into long songs of "what cheer, what cheer." Sam was not sure, but he was sure the 'what cheer' made the pines uneasy by all their shuddering, which caused more cones to fall. "Ouch!" said Henry, "I might avoid stepping on them, but not getting plucked from above." Henry rubbed his head, but then frantically started shaking his paws to remove whatever was then crawling on them.

Each cone that fell released a bevy of more insects sent scattering on the ground. "Run, you pestilence!" said a cardinal triumphantly. The cardinal, which had been on Mim, turned and looked at him and said, "Oh… a mockingbird, at first I thought you might be a potential new recruit with that red scarf around your neck." "I should sa sa say not. I am not ja ja joining your odd sa sa society… pa pah pretty boys," said Mim as he dusted himself off. "Looks like Will Scarlet 'Scarf' does not want to join our merry little band," said the Cardinal with a grin between its large hooked beak. All the cardinals broke into jovial laughter, and one patted Mim on the back. The cardinal, who first made his appearance known on the unsuspecting Mim, stepped forward and said, "My name is Ostap, and we are part of an underground movement to save the individual. Long live the revolution!"

# Chapter 14

# WE WILL SEE

# The Runt Oak

The three friends sat around and were engaged in a deep discussion. These three were not our three heroes currently in the Whispering Pines, and the discussion was not actually that deep, and frankly, it was pretty shallow, since there was a possum who thought he knew all the answers without having any.

"I tell you, Spurgeon, this situation is pretty prickly if you ask me," said the possum, talking to the porcupine. The porcupine's quills were at attention as he voiced his displeasure with the possum, "Well, your eyesight is not the greatest this time of day, and that jug in your hand does not help your position." "That's my point, my pointy friend… position, our position. Do we even have one?" cited the possum. "Then can someone tell me what position is the position we do not have, which we are looking for, Norman?" said Spurgeon back at the possum. "Our position is to do as my Uncle Cyrus instructed. The Colonel told my uncle, and he told me, and I am telling you," said the raccoon, now entering the conversation. "Tell us what, Louis? We've been sitting here doing nothing because nothing has been clearly defined as nothing, and I have nothing to say about it," said Norman, taking a sip from the jug.

Norman was about to say something (or rather some more of not a thing), but then let out a belch. Norman looked at Louis and then Spurgeon, "See the position you have put us in?" stated the possum. At this comment, one of Spurgeon's quills shot off in frustration. "Whatever the position, it needs to have a dam," answered the raccoon. "Where is this dam supposed to be built, and what are we going to build the dam with?" raged the porcupine as another errant quill shot off. "Yes, the dam that makes little sense, with no direction, which brings us back to the position, and that is a position I intend to uphold," said Norman. "Sure wish the beavers were here, they know a thing or three about dams," said Spurgeon. "Beavers? Their independent position cannot comprehend the whole. The last thing we need is a bunch of stubborn, bucktooth, squatters infringing on the position of others and then building a house on the position," detracted Norman. "Positions! Positions! You and your positions!" screamed Spurgeon, holding back another onslaught of quills as the pressure built up more than any dam they wanted to build.

It was really a wonder that Louis' uncle Cyrus ever won the county seat by the river bottom, when Norman was clearly the better politician who could defend positions nobody could ever hold him accountable for. Cyrus got the position because he kissed the Colonel's tail feathers, and not by merit. "Tarnation! Look at all those pesky bugs over there. If there ever was any position where that 'know-it-all' Colonel wanted us to build his dam, those termites of his surely took that answer to their stomachs," said Spurgeon, becoming even more disturbed about the entire business of a dam.

Bits of sad timber lay scattered along the dry river bottom, as bugs crawled from cracks in the ground and continued devouring the dam's material. The fragments of the aforementioned building material might have been able to tell them where they could build if not for the deteriorating condition of their deteriorated wood, arguing with their now growing multiple personalities upon separation. "There you go, boys, we are in no position to question the position… especially when the position is moving all along the position of said river bottom," said Norman, as he took another swig from the jug and another quill shot off from a frustrated Spurgeon.

Cyrus' nephew was feeling like a forgotten spoke on a third wheel. "Can't you see the position you are putting me in when my uncle asks, where is the dam the Colonel asked for?" worried Louis.

"We will see," said Norman, as all three turned back to look at the increasingly disappearing timber meant for the dam. "See what!" screamed Spurgeon, as the other two then screamed after a volley of quills flew off the porcupine.

Worlds seem to be the same all over the world, and even under and over the world into the world of another dimension. While Norman, Spurgeon, and Louis were complaining and getting nothing done for Cyrus and the Colonel (who would take credit, or not accept blame for what others did or did not do), it was a totally different situation back in the Whispering Pines. Sam, Mim, and Henry were actually trying to do something with all their might, while others (bugs, trees, and who knows what or who?) were criticizing their every move by every thought.

While the trio at the river bottom were in cahoots with the termites and getting nowhere, which was fine with them except for Louis, our three heroes and the rebel cardinals were doing all they could to stifle the menace and get somewhere… though they were not sure exactly where. The cardinals had been busy explaining the situation, which was not as it seemed. It was not the fault of the pines that made them say the devious things they did, but the bugs.

One also might say it wasn't even the bugs' fault. The little guys were not that bright, and at least people like the Colonel made them feel important. OK, if you believe that, then you're just being silly. As they say, ignorance does not grant innocence. Big, small, bright, or dull, there is never any excuse for making others feel small just to make yourself feel big. Now, back to those doing something which was not all about them, but seeing the importance in others.

As Ostap talked more about his assumptions and observations concerning their ongoing struggles against a whispering regime, more birds arrived. These were more subdued in color, as the red cardinals were vibrant and as humble as the red cardinals were proud. These new arrivals were actually cardinals themselves, female cardinals. Ostap seemed surprised by their presence and scolded them for putting themselves in danger by venturing too far from the sanctuary of their nests. However, one female cardinal ignored Ostap's self-righteous tone. "My dear Ostap, I will not accept such a tone of superiority from you. It is we who take care of your young while you are gallivanting around in the name of the 'revolution'. It is us who have to fend for ourselves while you are fending for others as these strangers. At least, allow us to contribute our part, because we are ultimately in this together."

With that, some of the female cardinals dropped a few bundles of leaves in front of the strangers. Sam cautiously unwrapped one leaf, making sure it too was not full of the whispering bugs. Opening the leaf, an ecstatic Mim proclaimed, "berries!!!" "Guide them where to go, by all means, Ostap, but please allow them to replenish their energy so they have enough strength to get there," beseeched the female cardinal.

Ostap turned his head to the side, sorry for how he had treated her. He slowly hopped over to her, and picking up one of the remaining bugs fleeing from the path, crushed it, and rubbed it on her feathers. "You glow, my dear, more beautiful than that fortuitous sunrise when I first saw you. Forgive me for my insolence. You are right, Eva," and the rest of the cardinals started singing the familiar "what cheer, what cheer".

Sam and his friends heartily ate the berries, and as the female cardinals were about to fly off, Ostap spoke to her again, "How is our young son?" "Proud of his father, as he should be," said Eva. Ostap was quiet, but one could tell her words had moved him deeply, and Eva, along with the other females, flew off. Ostap watched her soft, warm plumage disappear into the pines, leaving its warmth behind in his heart. He was proud. The best kind of pride, proud of someone he loved.

Nestling in his heart, Ostap reflected for a while and finally returned to the plight of his guests. "It might seem endless, but you are close to leaving the pines. The darkest paths always seem to be the longest. We will accompany you and do whistling for you to keep the whispers at bay," and with that, the party ventured on to the cardinals' protective serenade. Ostap had been right, it was not long till the pines became less numerous and the path momentarily sloped downwards from the higher terrain they had been previously on.

They were now on level ground, and the pines had given way to maple trees, which had lined the path. Sam and his companions welcomed the less confined space and took a deep breath from the air, which was now free of whispers. "Follow this path onward, my fellow brothers in arms. You will no longer have the whispers from the pines, but there is a new challenge ahead. It worries me where you go, but I will refrain from my concerns. Partly because I am not sure of what lies ahead, but only know what rumors suggest dwells there. Most of what we fear is often unwarranted fodder from the mind, which never comes true, but do be careful. Keep your wits about you for whatever you may or may not encounter… and be especially on guard once you notice the weeping fig trees," said a grave Ostap. "But can you give us at least a hint?" implored Sam. A spark of vigilant light came from eyes hidden behind the cardinal's black mask, and he ushered the word, "Bohdan."

The other cardinals who had been carrying on with chirps in the background went silent. "That is the same word we heard leaving the Sequoyah," said Sam. "It da duh did not sa sa sound so ba bah bad to me," said Mim. "Anything is better than those buggy pines, brother. I'm not scared of this 'Bohdan' you speak of," said a brave Henry. "We will see... We will see," said Ostap, and changing their mood, the cardinals became merry once again with their familiar devil-may-care attitude, leaving some courage behind as they flew off. "We will see," said Sam to himself, and the three seekers carried on.

# Chapter 15

# **BOHDAN**

# The Runt Oak

The maple people gave off a bittersweet impression, small talk avoiding a much bigger issue. Sam could feel a certain current of hopelessness running through them. This heavy strain, which weighed on the maples, reminded Sam of Ian and his mother when things were not going well. The memory of Ian's grandmother came to mind, those trying times, and how his pack had dealt with the agonizing downward spiral till she passed from their world. Like Ian and Vivian, the maples in their thoughts rambled endlessly about issues that were not at the heart of their worries; these worries were deeply rooted. A distraction to prevent asking the pertinent questions over and over, while making them feel they were doing something about something they had no control. One maple, for instance, kept talking about the state of a tuft of grass by the path, which appeared just fine to Sam, while another was talking about how a small stream, which was close by, was not close enough.

It was as if there was nothing to preoccupy their attention enough. Given any silence, they feared their actual feelings might cause them to break down crying. In essence, finding intrigue by watching the grass grow to avoid tears from falling down on the leaves that bore them. Mim seemed the least affected by this, since the thoughts of the maples were not much different from his own incoherent thoughts that steadily came out in odd tangents. The survival mechanism of the maples was a pastime Mim knew all too well.

While Sam could move along the path, distracted from the warning of Ostap by his own melancholia, Mim by his own familiar state of being reinforced by the maples, it was Henry whose courage was unwavering since they broke free of the pines. Henry was born blind. It was no mental affliction which impaired him, and he learned that feeling sorry for himself helped nothing. He had enough already going against him then to let himself be his own worst enemy by throwing a pity party in his own honor. Henry's survival mechanism kicked in, and the fragile recourse of the maples made him kick back even stronger. Henry would take off down the path, disappear, and then reappear, becoming a movable picket for his tiny army of three. After a couple of hours, the reconnaissance of Henry became commonplace, with his reports of "all's clear, my brothers".

It was late afternoon when Henry arrived, and this time, his scouting mission brought back something different. The news was not too encouraging, simply because Henry said he smelled pine trees again. Sam did not like the idea of having to whistle all over again to stifle those insidious bugs, and then there was the mysterious Colonel, whom Ostap never fully explained. "Are you sure there are pines ahead?" said Sam, hoping Henry had been mistaken. "Well," said Henry, "they smelled close enough to be pines to me, and look what I stepped on… again!" And with that, Henry showed them a cone. "Yeah, I see what you mean," said Sam, disheartened.

Mim hopped over to the cone and inspected it with his beak, and after a minute of deliberation, said, "Na nah no ba bah bugs, Na nah not one trace of a ahhh ba bug." Sam smelled the cone and could not find any evidence that it had ever had bugs in it. "Did you hear anything? You know… any foul whispering?" questioned Sam of Henry. "No, brother, not one single irritating word," replied Henry. "This does not change our path, and I do not intend to whistle all over again unless we absolutely have to. Plus, last time brought cardinals, but this time might bring something altogether different in this place… and maybe something we do not want to attract," thought Sam. "A ba bah Bohdan?" said a nervous Mim. "That too," said Sam, as he surveyed the path from which Henry had just come. "Well, if there is a Bohdan, and whatever a Bohdan is, we might as well get it over with and meet it," decided Henry. "True enough," said Sam as he motioned them forward. "Spa spah speak for your sa sah self," stammered Mim as he reluctantly followed his friends.

Henry then took off in front as before, ignoring the protests from Sam that they should stick together. "I came back in one piece; there were no bugs in that cone, and who is to say these pines are bad? Some kind of scout I would be, if when needed most, I would skedaddle before finding any actual danger," shouted Henry farther up ahead and vanishing down the path.

The maples diminished along the path, and the dark spirals of evergreen ahead seemed to suggest that Henry's observation of pines had been right. Entering the grove, Sam looked at the trees and noticed that there was something different about them. They looked like pines, but something was not quite right about them. These trees appeared different. Sam turned his nose up and inhaled deeply. "They smell different from pines," said Sam, studying the scent. "Da duh that is ba bah because they are na nah not pines, they are fa fah firs," said Mim.

Mim was right; these were fir trees and not pines. At this moment, Henry returned. "We are over here!" said Sam, raising his voice in order that Henry could place them sooner. "See, there must have been a truce among the spruce, because these pines have no bugs and no bad words," said Henry, catching his breath. "We have caught on that they are firs, Henry, not pines," corrected Sam. "Oh please, brother, I do not think it is really necessary for me to grab onto your fur again," protested Henry. "Na nah no no no, ta tah trees, ta trees, fir people, ha huh Henry!" demanded Mim. "Oh… what is a fir tree?" said Henry, a little embarrassed. "They look like pines, Henry, but they are not pines. Looks can deceive," confirmed Sam.

# Bohdan

The three looked up at the firs as they rose around them, attempting to rid themselves of any preconceived thoughts. First off, even if they had been pines, Henry was right that it did not mean all pines were bad. Lastly, just because the firs resembled pines did not mean they should be judged by bad pines. Only a fool judges the individual by the whole, and this includes trees… though Sam sometimes found it hard to find the good in a thorny hackberry, though the birds in his backyard did not find it hard at all eating the marvelous berries of the generous hackberry trees.

They carried on along the path, knowing now these were firs and not pines. Sam, after a while, realized, just because the firs appeared quiet did not mean they were not saying something. Sam remembered when Anton called the pines his wayward brothers, and if it were not for the bugs, the pines would have been relatively quiet, too. The firs, pines, and Sequoyah acted as listeners. Setting these three apart, the giant sequoias, unlike the other two, were active listeners. The firs seemed not to want to offer anything of themselves. Sam knew they were listening, because he got the same feeling one gets when you feel someone is watching you and felt the firs inquisitive attention.

There is an old proverb that says a man who goes to town and says nothing to anyone is actually saying a lot about themselves, and these fir trees were no different. While the Sequoyah cared, the pines and firs did not give any indication they cared at all. Maybe, it might have been that the fir thought themselves too aloof to bother with the strangers they viewed below (though the strangers did literally walk below their tall shadows). Be it they didn't care or thought they were better, both views were disturbing to Sam and his inherent tail wagging demeanor- the firs talking behind their backs from behind their bark. So, under this judgmental quiet, the three walked. It was dark under the thick frames of the fir, and such silence has a way of muffling one's own thoughts and feels rather loud.

There was a slight break in the foliage above, and in between the open points of the firs, Sam and Mim noticed the sun was going down. They could hear Henry's familiar pitter-patter coming towards them, but then they heard him yell, "It's dreadful, just breaks the heart!" Once Henry collected himself, he told them what he heard and felt. "It was so sad, so, so sad. So many voices crying out, some soft and some wailing uncontrollably," said Henry, emotionally still shaken. "Who was crying? Henry, who was crying and why?" said Sam, who also became distraught not only by the squirrel's words but also by Henry's now broken courage. "It's oh oh OK, Henry. It's OK, we are with you," said Mim equally affected.

Henry then took a deep breath and managed a slight smile, feeling the comfort of his friends. From under his hat, Henry then handed them some fruit. "I managed to secure this before I was affected, so. Those poor trees, their soft leaves and bark overpouring with sorrow." Mim looked at the fruit, "fa fah figs." Sam then remembered what Ostap had told them at their parting: "be especially on guard once you notice the weeping fig trees."

Henry did not take off ahead now and didn't need Sam to tell him to grab onto his fur again. He took hold willingly. Walking in the darkness of night and under the canopy of the diminishing firs they heard the moaning of much sorrow. Then Sam heard a voice come from one fir where their number made way for other trees ahead, "Judge by your instincts, son of Vovk, not by what you see." Sam waited for more, but there was no more. With each sniffle along the path, the weeping figs and their sadness soon surrounded them. It was the kind of pain which makes thoughts incoherent. All three wanted to offer solace to their poor people, but they could not find the words as the figs could not find theirs.

All three held onto each other tightly, enduring the lamentations of the weeping figs. As they left soft prints behind, the damp ground seemed fitting, as if the path had been littered with tears. The path then curved away from the weeping figs and went behind large rock formations that held more fir trees. The party could then hear running water, and from the sides of the rock formations, they saw little springs of water run down. At the bottom of the falls, where there were ferns growing, they could hear them arguing, "This water is mine", "No, it is my water", "This water is too warm", "This water is too cold", and "I don't want your water". Though the ferns seemed rather serious about their objections, their small, delicate structure made their verbal altercations comical. Sam and his friends could not help but chuckle at the trivial minor disagreements among the little ferns. After the overwhelming sorrow of the weeping figs, this was a welcomed change. Henry then even seemed to get his courage back and let go of Sam's fur. As they moved past the ferns, they noticed the now rocky path ascending. Being careful not to slip on the wet surface, they slowly made their way to the crest of the path and, looking over, saw… a cave.

The cave was rather large, and its entrance extended outwards towards the path which went past it. They studied the cave for a while and talked among themselves about what they should do next, when Henry then said, "Let me feel my way around the backside of the cave if it is possible. By what you tell me, the entrance runs rather close to the path. Don't think it would be too smart walking in full view of that entrance, because who knows what might be inside? If I can find a way around it, I will come back and we can then avoid any unnecessary risk." Sam did not like the idea of Henry going alone around the cave, but Mim did not help the situation by agreeing, after Henry put the fear of the unknown in him. Henry slid off to the right, and even though he was blind, he had the agile ability of his kind to feel his way easily through the assorted protruding roots and rocks.

A few minutes after Henry had left, Sam and Mim noticed something moving inside of the cave. Whatever was moving, it was big… real big. From out of the darkness of the cave came a foot- a really big foot. "Sa suh Sasquatch!" said Mim in an emphatic gasp to Sam. Out of the darkness, another large foot appeared. Soon, the two large feet were joined by equally large reptilian legs, an elongated big belly with arms connected to claws, wings, and rising up a long neck which bent under the top of the entrance, revealing a magnificent but frightening, scaled head. This was no Sasquatch, and if he had not been present in real time, Sam would have loved to have shown it to Ian. Sam had seen this creature before in Ian's books, his movies, and on the mantle where Ian was always reapplying its long tail that broke off. This was no Bigfoot. This was a dragon!

The dragon was huge, and its scales were the color of dark midnight purple. As the moonlight shone down on him, the scales gave an iridescent violet shine, which reflected off the sides of the dripping wet cave rock. Sam and Mim were too frightened to move, awestruck and scared senseless. The dragon, on the other hand, had no such issues and moved out onto the path. Once on the path, he stretched out his wings and let out a yawn, which sent a rising cloud from out of his nostrils. Sam and Mim felt a chill, not only because they were scared, but it suddenly became really cold. The dragon then turned and started to walk down the path away from the cave in the opposite direction from them. Both breathed a sigh of relief till they remembered something… "Henry!!!"

# Chapter 16

# THEN THERE WAS FOUR

# The Runt Oak

Henry was making good time, feeling his way around the rocks, and by the circumference of his movements, felt assured he was getting around the structure which made up the cave. The rocks leveled towards the bottom, and he knew he was getting close to the opposite side. The air was very humid from all the natural springs, which could be heard along the walls of the formations he was covering, but then it suddenly became very cold. As Henry was reaching his leg across to follow a descending ledge towards the bottom, the sudden cold made his leg cramp up, and he lost his traction on the moss-encrusted rocks, sliding uncontrollably to the bottom.

"Well, that is the quick way to do it," said Henry to himself, as he then went headfirst into a large tree which seemed to have moved in front of him. Henry tried to feel around this tree, which bared his movement, and it had the strangest roots. The roots were smooth and extremely hard, with points at the end that did not seem to go underground. Henry climbed up one of the roots to the trunk, and that too was strange. The trunk had more texture, but still felt firmer than any tree he had ever felt before. Another fascinating aspect of this trunk was that the texture was very contrived, with a definite pattern. The closest thing Henry ever felt before to this was a snake, but these scales were far sturdier. Then he noticed the strangest thing of all. This tree started moving. "Hmmm, a pointy root, scales, moving… this is no tree!" said Henry to himself, and he fainted.

Sam and Mim looked down into the cave, staring towards where the path continued onward behind its rock formation. "I heard something," said Sam, as he turned his head to the side and his ears perked up. "Uh I I I da duh did not ha hear anything?" said Mim, full of worry. "It was a long scraping noise, and then I heard nothing else," said Sam, trying to discern what was taking place out of view. Dogs have acute hearing, as they do smell, and Sam was sure of what he heard. "Ma mah maybe, the da duh dragon has hu Henry… ma muh maybe he is ka kah carving him up to… uh… eat!" gasped Mim in horror. Sam's mind and heart were on Henry, too, but he was sure of what he didn't smell, that being blood, and was sure he did not hear any sounds of distress, either. The fact of the matter was, regardless of what was going on, Henry had not returned yet, and no good could come from them just staying put. They wouldn't be able to help Henry if he needed them from behind the rock they were currently at, and they wouldn't be able to continue down the path just sitting there.

Henry came to and found himself lying on what felt, this time, surely against a tree. Every so often, he felt an icy breeze, and the breeze had a rhythm to it. The rhythm which had been the act of breathing, then spoke in a deep voice, "Are you alright, little one? What do they call you? My name is… Bohdan."

"Bohdan, did you say Bohdan?" said Henry, realizing he was now face to face with the enigma behind the name. "Yes, my name is Bohdan. I know it is a strange name, for I have never encountered another here by such a name. It is a name of the Old World. Maybe I am old, too? I don't know, because I do not go out much and seem to sleep my life away. I have a nice cave, though, and have treasure worth protecting. But please tell me, what is your name? It would be nice to talk to someone new, and not these willow oaks who never tell me anything new except to remind me where to stay, so I and my treasure can be safe. They mean well, I guess? But they are rather boring," said the dragon to the blind squirrel, who was not aware of what he was.

"My name is Henry. Just Henry, and have met a few fellow Henrys in my time, so I guess I can't be too old. Look, I am sure your cave is very nice, and your treasure must be something special, but there is a formidable creature about, and I have friends who need me. So, if you don't mind, I think it best I go on my way. Don't think I could offer anything interesting to talk about, anyway. You see, I cannot see. I am blind, so my experiences are rather limited, too. You have your limited space in and around your cave, and me my limited senses," said Henry, being polite and feeling now in a hurry.

There was quiet, and Henry was then afraid he had upset Bohdan, and he apologized in case he had said anything wrong. Henry waited for a response and clutched his arms about himself, for it had become freezing when Bohdan was speaking. Then Henry heard two familiar voices filled with apprehension. "Leave him be. We mean you no harm, and did not mean to disturb you. If it would not be asking too much, we should be on our way and will leave you in peace," said Sam between being polite and begging. Mim, losing his wits, as the dragon turned to face them, shouted at Henry, "ga gah get over ha here, it's a da duh dragon!"

At the word dragon, Henry attempted to make his way quickly to the sound of his friends, but only ran into Bohdan again (Bohdan was quite large). To the horror of Sam and Mim, Bohdan picked up Henry. To their surprise, the dragon turned to them, walked over, and with an ample space between them, softly put Henry down next to his friends. "Thank you. Now, if we may, we really must be going," said an astonished Sam, as they cautiously started making their way around the dragon.

When they were on the other side of the dragon, Henry stopped. Something did not feel right to him because nothing about Bohdan felt wrong. "It was nice meeting you, Bohdan, and we wish you a good day," said Henry, feeling right about his manners. "Bohdan… did you say Bohdan?" said a mystified Sam. Mim tried to say something, but was too interested in the freedom the path had to offer away from the dragon. "Please don't wish me a good day. I have nothing good… I don't even have good dreams. You would only leave me with nothing," said Bohdan with a sincerity that melted the frigid chill which surrounded them.

Dogs have an intuition: they can feel when someone is bad, and Sam did not feel any bad. The fir tree had reminded him of this before, the sorrow of the weeping figs, and now it took a blind squirrel to remind him that what you see can be deceiving. Much to the chagrin of Mim, Henry followed Sam as he walked back towards the dragon. Bohdan was then in as much of a shock as Sam and Mim when they first saw him exit the cave. While Sam and Mim had been shocked with fear, Bohdan was shocked by joy. "My name is Sam. A lot of people keep calling me son of Vovk, but I have never even met the guy. This bird is Mim, and this squirrel is Henry," said Sam, introducing him and his companions. "Henry, I know, now I know you, and let it be known I am Bohdan… oh wait, and I do have something good, please stay awhile, and come to my cave and let me show you," said the overjoyed dragon. Sam and Henry followed the dragon along with the apprehensive Mim. The three made sure to give Bohdan some ample room, since the dragon's long tail was wagging like Sam himself when happy.

Bohdan lowered his head as he entered his cave, as the others followed. There was a steady stream of water from above the cave, which sent cold water onto the companions as they hurried in, attempting to avoid getting doused. Once inside, the cave opened up and was much larger than anyone of them could have expected- and far tidier than anyone could have expected.

This was a well-kept cave, and dare one say, resembled more of a house than a cave. When Sam started to shake the water off from entering, Bohdan reminded him to be careful and not get the floor wet. This cave was immaculate because Bohdan kept it so. They followed Bohdan down what seemed a dimly lit high hallway, and as they went further, it opened up into an immense space. It was if someone constructed a cathedral inside, and beams of light somehow found their way in from above, revealing a spotless interior. Walking under the magnificence of the cavern roof in awe, Bohdan retraced their steps with an oddly constructed mop and cleaned up after them. This was like no dragon Sam had ever read about in Ian's books. "I spend a lot of time inside, and cleaning is just something I have developed a penchant for over the years," said Bohdan, as he returned the mop to a corner where there were various other mops and brooms. On further inspection, this cave seemed more like a mansion than a house.

Bohdan then tossed them a large towel, about the size of a good-sized camping tent. Unable to grab it, the towel fell over them, and Mim squawked, "I ca cah can't see!" Henry responded, "I can't either." Sam grabbed the towel with his teeth and, after more than a little effort, was able to pull it off of them. "What is this for?" asked Sam of Bohdan. "Please clean your feet. I am going to show you my treasure room." Sam thought to himself, "This dragon keeps a cleaner cave than the veterinarian hospital they make me go to." The three made a token effort to clean their feet, treating the towel as a rug, and followed Bohdan into one of the arched adjoining rooms, which lined the main room of the cavern. Walking into the room, a blaze of colorful light bounced all around.

The rest of the cavern, unlike this room, had been evenly carved. Instead, it resembled more of what one might have expected in the structure of a cave, but the structure was the only thing one would have considered normal. The entire room was made of gold. The walls, the rocks jutting from the surface, were all gold. Everything sparkled in golden rainbow hues. If Mim would have been a raven, he would have been having a greedy conniption fit with all the shiny colors that he would have been unable to pick up. "This is my one good thing. This is my treasure. Its value is limitless. I have been told so by the willow oaks," said Bohdan, as he inspected the room for anything which might need cleaning.

Sam looked about the room, and then something struck him as odd. Vivian's golden ring from her grandmother was made of gold, but it did not shine in such multiple hues as this gold. Maybe it was magic gold, thought Sam, and he went closer to study it. Sam had seen this before in Ian's room, and it was not gold but iron pyrite… fool's gold.

Sam's facial expression became gloomy; he found it hard within himself to tell Bohdan his good thing was not so good after all. Bohdan looked at Sam and spoke, "What is wrong? Did you find a smudge or some dirty area to be cleaned?" Sam felt he might as well tell him the truth, and simply said, "This gold has no value, because it is not even gold, but an ore that resembles gold." Bohdan then did something completely unexpected: he started laughing hysterically. "I am not joking with you about your good thing. I wouldn't dare do that to you. This is fool's gold," said Sam in a serious tone. Bohdan kept laughing though, and when he had controlled his laughter, said, "It figures, I believe you. It is hard for a dragon to read a plant's mind for the truth, but it is easy for us to read other living creatures. It's in the eyes," said Bohdan. Bohdan and Sam then noticed that Henry and Mim were no longer in the room. Walking back into the main cavern, they found Henry and Mim wrapped in the large towel Bohdan had thrown on them.

"Ca cah cold, brrrrr," shivered Mim. "That was me. You see, I am a frost dragon. I apologize for my laughter when in the room, but I could not help myself. Laughing at one's self is the best kind of laughter. Up close and personal jokes are always closer to the heart where true mirth resides," said Bohdan, and as he was about to laugh again, caught himself and covered his mouth with his talons. "Amen, I do that all the time, brother," said Henry, laughing. "Well, I still have a good thing I could show you, though it is not in my cave and it is not mine," invited Bohdan, as he motioned them to follow him back outside.

They walked outside, and as they were leaving the threshold of the cave, Bohdan stopped. "What is wrong?" said Henry, as he noticed the heavy footfalls of Bohdan become quiet. Then they could feel the willow oaks speaking outside his cave. "Where do you think you are going?" "Just was going to show them something good," said Bohdan in a subdued voice. "All that is good is in your cave dragon, plus it is not safe venturing so far out," said another one of the willow oaks.

Mim then spoke up, "You are ba bah big, nobody would ta tah try ca cah can hurt you even if they wa wah wanted to." Bohdan was about to have a nervous breakdown and was acting nothing like the dragon they had spoken to before. "I can't co it. I don't know why… why I can't do it?" said Bohdan, and he actually started to sob. "Oh, yes, you can, Bohdan. Grab Sam's fur, that is what I do," encouraged Henry as Sam's eyes got really large, thinking about the dragon's talons digging into his flesh. Timidly, Bohdan touched Sam's fur with the tip of one of his claws. "Are we going or what?" said Henry cheerfully, and Sam, Mim, Henry, and Bohdan started walking forward.

The willow oaks were beside themselves. This was unthinkable to them. The willow oaks started to rustle and lose leaves, being in more shock than either Bohdan or his companions that day. Unable to stop the dragon, one willow oak threatened, "The ferrets, what about the ferrets? Your only friends who visit you. What will they say… or even more importantly, what will they tell others?" More objections were cast by the willow oaks, but they were drowned out by Mim, who ranted about how one should never trust the words of an oak with stringy leaves. After all, where is the strength oaks are known for in that? The willow oaks, with no success, felt them move away up the path. Little did those willow oaks know... Bohdan would never clean that cave again.

Bohdan got his legs under him, and his strides lengthened as he started to believe in himself. The dragon actually started moving a little too fast, and the rest had to slow him down. Not only had Bohdan been moving too fast, but they could feel a noticeable incline to the path. Bohdan stopped, waiting for the others to catch up. When Sam and his companions caught up, the dragon tucked his wings in and pointed with excitement to his left towards a narrow path leading off the path. "The good thing is close! Can't you smell and hear the good?" said Bohdan, beaming with anticipation.

They followed the dragon and a scent of freshness, while the sound of rushing water could be heard. Reaching the edge, they were amazed to see a beautiful waterfall cascading into a large pool of water far down below. "Jump on my back! It is your turn to hold on to me and find courage… find wonder and something good," said a giddy Bohdan. At first, they were a little hesitant, but the good-natured dragon insisted. Bohdan turned to Mim, who was acting reluctant, mainly because he was smaller than the others and finding it difficult to jump onto the dragon's back without sliding off his smooth scales, "No problem, you have wings and can just follow me down," said Bohdan, unaware of Mim's condition. The very thought of flying gave Mim an extra rush of energy, and he grabbed hold of Henry's tail, flipping onto the back of the dragon with the others.

Bohdan opened his wings, and unlike the gaunt of his heavy steps, he flew gracefully down, not much different than the grace of a hippo once underwater swimming, to the edge of the twinkling pool below. At the bottom, looking up, they realized how high the waterfall was, and also how beautiful this glittering natural spectacle was. Bohdan went to the edge of the pool and looked into the water, which became like a mirror. The other three joined him, and what they witnessed could only be explained in the heart. There are certain kinds of happiness which cannot be described but only felt, and all four felt deeply.

Bodhan looked in and saw an ancient tree; it was a tall baobab tree. Roosted on top was Bohdan, but roosted to his left and right were two other dragons, a blue frost dragon and a red fire drake. "Mama, Papa, it is your Bohdan," cried the dragon as icy tears of joy melted in the pool below. Mim looked in and saw himself flying with his family. Sam looked in and saw Ian and Vivian sitting with him outside on their porch. Finally, Henry the blind squirrel saw himself, and what he felt glowed so much from inside that it would engulf any attempt to describe the happiness his other two friends felt. Then the reflections of joy slowly faded, and Bohdan said, "Something good."

"But how?" said Sam to Bohdan. "How? One cannot explain love and the magic it creates," said the dragon. Bohdan said the pool only reads the love in the heart for a few beats, because it is from the heart that magic and love can be found. Once the pool reads what your heart longs for, it cannot show for long, because the heart would be in danger of racing so fast and feeling so much happiness. "Will the image return once the heart calms down?" said Henry softly. "I am afraid not. After the pool reads you, it is content to reveal your joy and not becoming it. You would have to wait many years to see it again. Once the heart is reminded of what it loves, it takes hundreds of years till it needs to be quenched again, and still it might not, because one never forgets real love. I have not been here for years untold, the willow oaks saw to that," spoke a solemn Bohdan.

Bohdan then said they must leave and respect the grace they had been given. The dragon led them to a path which skirted away from the waterfall and magical pool. They passed numerous alder trees, seeming to be in deep mediation. "They are not like the other trees with their issues, for their mind exists in another plane not open to the worries found here. It is sad, though, for to feel in the other world, they are unable to actually experience this one. They're caught between nowhere and everywhere," Bohdan declared. As Sam walked along, he could feel the soothing vibration of the alder's chants.

The party followed a wide ledge which seemed to wrap around a hill. When they reached the top, Sam and his friends discovered they must have been slowly scaling a mountain since entering the Whispering Pines. Looking out, they saw a vast expanse stretching for miles. This strange place, which Sam had no name for, was stunning. From here, Sam could definitely 'see the forest from the trees'; he could see all the forests. Bohdan pointed to the path which led down to the other side of the mountain. "I am not going back to those willow oaks, their shady ferrets, or my cave and its false value. Please, take me with you?" said Bohdan. All three smiled at the dragon, and Mim said, "Wa wha we would na nah not want it any uh other way." Bohdan then told them to get on his back again. "Why did you show us the path if you were just going to fly us down Bohdan?" said Sam. "I was not sure you would want me, but now I know you will. Bohdan has found something good. So much good… you, you and you."

# Chapter 17

# THE PARADIGM IS A SHIFTING

# The Runt Oak

The bugs along the branches of the Deadwood Tree held on, bracing themselves for another quake under the roots of the tree. They had dealt with the winds of change before, but this was more than a mood change. The last couple of days had become very tedious for the tree and the Colonel's state of mind. The very foundation of the tree and the owl's contrived sense of control were eroding at an accelerated rate. A screech was heard from inside the outside hovel of a house, the frequency of which caused some bugs to fall and be thankful for their exoskeleton.

"Darn blasted, this is not the bathroom!" yelled the owl, and he let out another screech, which caused Cyrus the raccoon to almost drop his pipe while in the process of lighting it. "I don't even know where I am anymore!" yelled the Colonel. "Open this door, Cyrus! Do something, would you? I need to find the bathroom?" said the owl, now banging on the door. This house on the Deadwood had a strange construction. Every time there was a massive shift, it would alter the house's physical reality. Now, the sporadic gusts of wind would only cause minor problems for the Colonel. Objects in his house might change position and meaning to him, but these quakes would change the very location of the rooms. The house was falling apart along with the Colonel's ability to control his illusion that dictated his own reality, which he imposed on others.

Cyrus put his pipe down and rushed to the door of the room where the owl had presently been having a fit. Approaching the door of the room where the Colonel's panic had originated from, there was another quake which sent the raccoon sliding into the door. Upon slamming into the door, the jarred door opened. Cyrus looked inside and did not find the Colonel, but found a toilet and a sink. With sounds of banging on a door, the owl was then heard from the opposite side of the house, now trapped in another room.

Mimicking the owl's mental state, this house held multiple rooms which went beyond one's first impression. Cyrus then, getting up from the floor, crawled on his hands and knees as he often did for the Colonel's demands, to the owl's new location in the strange house. When Cyrus opened the door, the Colonel burst out and knocked him down again in a rush. "Where is the confounded restroom?" yelled the Colonel. Cyrus pointed to the room where the owl had been a while ago. The Colonel let out another screech and slammed the door as he took care of his business.

Things then appeared stable for the time being, as the owl exited the bathroom, acting overly dignified, as if nothing ever happened. "Sorry, Colonel," said Cyrus as he sat down again on the chair which was now facing the owl's desk in a totally different direction. The Colonel started walking where he expected his desk to be from his last recollection, only to find it had moved to his study. He momentarily paused, and then, acting as if he meant to go in the other direction, picked up a book he had never read, which had fallen off the shelf.

"As I thought… imbeciles," said the Colonel, pretending some idea on the page he was not looking at was wrong. "I really hope this is the last of them dreadful shakes for now," said Cyrus as he picked up his pipe, which now had become an envelope opener. "What shakes? That never happened?" said the owl in denial. "What do you mean, Colonel, just a while ago you…" But before Cyrus could finish, the Colonel cut him off. "What are you, crazy?" said the manipulative owl. "I am not crazy… I think?" said Cyrus, now doubting his own reality. "Thinking is the last thing you should burden yourself with trying to do. For instance, explain why you have that envelope opener in your mouth?" said the owl.

# The Runt Oak

Cyrus, in a confused state, noticed that this was the case, and then wiped off some blood from his upper lip caused by the opener. "You really need help. You need a therapist or, even worse, I would recommend you see a physician. Your kind carries rabies, you know? And, this might be the first sign of the affliction," chided the Colonel. Cyrus, with a worried expression, doubting his only reality, fumbled around his waistcoat as he found his side pocket to place the handkerchief back, which he had been using to wipe his lip.

There was then a scratching on the front door. "Go see who it is?" said the Colonel to Cyrus. Cyrus got up, and upon looking through the peephole of the door, could see no one. "There is nobody there?" said Cyrus. "Well, it sure cannot be one of the bugs," said the agitated owl. A face then momentarily appeared in front of the peephole and went down, and then reappeared again as it jumped up to be seen. "It is one of the ferrets jumping up and down," said Cyrus. "Then open the door! They really should invent a game where one can hammer them on their head when they do that irritating jumping," scathed the Colonel.

The ferret frantically rushed in and went up to the Colonel, causing Cyrus to fall yet once again as he scurried around him. "If you start foaming at the mouth, Cyrus, I will have no option but to shoot you and put you out of your misery," said the Colonel with a menacing look. "So, what are you doing here? And it better be good," said the Colonel impatiently. "He is gone, Colonel. The willow oaks said he just walked off with some strangers and did not return," said the ferret. "What! Just walked off! Why didn't the willow oaks go after him?" said the Colonel in a building rage. "Trees can't walk, sir," said the ferret, shaking before the owl. "Where were your people, you rodent?" said the Colonel, now seething with anger. The ferret tried to respond, but became so frightened he could not talk. "Incompetence!!!" shouted the Colonel, letting out a horrible shriek. "Leave me, you worthless piece of driftwood! Before I put meat on my menu tonight, starting with you," the owl sneered.

At this, the ferret took off like a shot, while another quake shook the house. Cyrus, who had placed himself up against the wall to avoid the ferret's hasty retreat, then fell backwards through an open room which was not there a moment ago. Cyrus got up, and thought what was good for the ferret was also the better part of valor for him, and went to leave too. "Not you, Cyrus, get back here and stop falling down. You are no better than that alcoholic nephew of yours, Louis, who hangs out with that good-for-nothing possum," belittled the Colonel. Cyrus went back to sit down after he located the chair. For now, the furniture was facing in yet another direction.

"That dragon, that stranger, those two oddballs. I will show them and put an end to this. I knew this would happen, but only my just clemency had prevented me from doing what I should have done a long time ago. How can a society function when you have people that won't adhere to the status quo? Individuality is a virus which must be eradicated. They don't belong." "Maybe you should have had your bugs pay closer attention?" said Cyrus with regret, thinking the Colonel might become upset that he was questioning him again. "I did, you idiot! You really are arrogant, Cyrus. The next thing I will find out is that Louis has not built that dam at the rate your lethargic mind is going. If you would ever care to listen to me, maybe you would learn something and earn your seat of authority, which my generosity alone granted you. I had sent the bugs, but between the dragon crushing them while cleaning and his cold air freezing them to death, they were of no use. That is why I sent the ferrets, but they are no different from any other weasel. I can't trust anyone, it seems," and then the Colonel dipped his head under his wings, exhausted from his tirade.

Cyrus was too scared to say anything, and surely would not say anything about the dam which had not been built. Sitting there, too scared to move, Cyrus waited. The raccoon wasn't sure, since the house on the Deadwood Tree was always in a state of darkness, but if there still was enough daylight, there might still be time to get that dam built or suffer the consequences, which might include his position on the county seat. In the uneasy silence of this corrupted owl's lair, he heard the steady breathing of the Colonel. It was still day, and the owl, being nocturnal, had fallen asleep.

Silently, Cyrus got up from the chair and tiptoed out of the house. Lifting his head moments later after the raccoon had gone, the Colonel woke up. His eyes had become dark like those of a shark, but deep within them, one could see a distant flame. "I will show them. I will get my control back, and all will be the same again. Everyone will be forced to act the same again," and with that, the Colonel went back to dreaming of their demise. Incidentally, the book the Colonel had used earlier as a prop to cloak his fragile ego would have served him well if he had actually read it. It was an old book about Buddhist monks. Within was a warning, "those who seek revenge dig two graves, one for the victim and one for themselves."

# Chapter 18

# LIKE A SPARK TO A BLAME

# The Runt Oak

Ian woke up groggy, lost in tired thought, as he made his way downstairs. He had a hard time sleeping since Sam had gone missing, and his body had eventually given in to a nap after he was barely able to make it through the morning. Naps in the afternoon often have the strangest dreams. Afternoon dreams are like scripts which had not made the cut for the nightly episode. One then realizes why they did not make the light of day when the light of day brings them forward. Once downstairs, Ian could not find his mom inside and then noticed her familiar arm holding a cup of coffee on the back porch from the side of the kitchen window. Walking out to join his mom, he noticed the smell of wood burning. "Don't tell me Uncle Jake is out front barbequing again? He might as well move his grill to the back with how often he comes by to do it," said Ian. Vivian smiled; this kind of small talk about a problem which was not really a problem was something they both needed to get their minds off of Sam.

Vivian's eyes fixated on the little oak in the backyard, and the smell of smoke made her imagine the druids she had told her husband would show up if he dared to light that little tree on fire. "He is good at it, Mom, don't get me wrong, but even a caveman would beg for some variety… Mom? Are you listening?" said Ian, as Vivian stared beyond what was not there. "Oh… what? Ah, no son, it is just the Fergusons burning brush across the street," said Vivian, as her vivid imagination took the cue and doubled down on the druid theme it found so interesting. "Of course! The Fergusons!! With a Gaelic name like that, they would love to summon those pesky druids," thought Vivian to herself, as she started laughing. Ian smiled to see his mother laugh. Vivian hardly ever smiled for a few years till

Greg eventually left their lives, and when she did, it seemed forced to satisfy those around her and never genuine.

They both then stared out into the distance past their yard, becoming mesmerized by the swaying tips of the pines that encompassed the empty lot in the back of their yard. Vivian then got up from her chair. "I'll be right back. I am going to call the fire department and make sure those druids got permission, since that burn ban is probably still in effect. We had some rain, but hardly enough with how dry it has been this summer. Just imagine what would happen if a spark got to those pines. The whole neighborhood would be encircled," and with that, she went inside. Ian turned his gaze back towards the pines, and then his day nap came back to him. It was, as I said, a strange dream, and those naps during the day can be so vivid. It had been like a dream within a dream. He had been flying over the pines and suddenly had found himself looking into a pool. When he had looked into the pool, he saw Sam, but stranger still, Sam was not alone. Ian saw a bird with a scarf, a squirrel with a floppy hat, and, of all things, a dragon.

This had not scared Ian. It actually made him extremely happy in the dream, and Sam and all the strange creatures were smiling back at him. When Ian had called out to Sam in the dream, he had then awoken. Ian snapped out of his reflection when the smell of brush burning gave way to the smell of fresh coffee as his mom walked past him back to her chair with a second cup.

Bohdan and his new friends descended below, looking for the path. Breaking free of the clouds, the land below was still barely visible. At first, it was expected to be mist since they were close to the Sequoyah, according to Bohdan's recollection. Though he had not taken flight in quite some time, this made little sense to him. Getting closer, as they skimmed above the treetops in the mist, they realized two things: these were not Sequoyah, and this was not mist. Yes, they were close to the Sequoyah, but these were the whispering pines, and this was… smoke!

Navigating through the smoke, the dragon somehow found traces of the path below and found a small clearing in the dense forest. Upon landing, they noticed a creature racing towards them. It was a weasel holding a lit torch, moving frantically in one direction and then to another. The weasel then noticed them, and his eyes had a crazed look.

"Never give a ferret what a weasel can do; they and their long fur have but little use. Never give an otter what a weasel can do; their childish ways will waste the light of day. It is what it is, and a weasel has no qualms about doing what it takes, taking it from you," recited the weasel in a mad state of euphoria.

The weasel then vanished off the path with only the light of his torch crackling in the distance, along with his insane ramblings. Soon, the party could see more torch lights bobbing in the darkness of the pines and the sinister voices of more weasels. A voice was then felt, and it was not a weasel. "We were so naïve, so foolish, so lazy, and so weak. Please help us," expressed the broken voice. "Oh, please, help us," joined another voice. Distraught voices filled the air. It was the pines, and they were no longer whispering but pleading from the depths of their roots.

Despite the tenuous situation which was unfolding around them, the companions had no choice but to go forward. One direction seemed just as good as the other for the want of finding a way out. The acrid smell of the pines catching on fire, and their haunting cries for help, made their progress almost as unbearable as the danger of the flames themselves, which seemed to increase. Sam turned one last time to see if maybe they should turn around and go back the way they came, but the path they had been on seemed even more hazardous than what lay ahead.

If it were not for the icy breath of Bohdan, their situation would have been most dire. Still, when his cold breath countered the flames, the resulting smoke made it impossible to see where they were going. Not being able to see was nothing new to Henry, and he took the lead upfront. Between the instincts of Henry and the cold escort of Bohdan, they might have a chance. Henry was then pushed down by another one of the weasels, which had come running across, taunting him, "What is wrong, squirrel? Got your chestnuts in the fire?" The demented weasel then screamed as he ran into a burning branch that fell on top of him.

Burning branches started to fall at an increased rate, along with the desperate pleas of the pines. Cautiously, they quickened their pace till Henry came to an abrupt stop, running into something which seemed to have burrowed out of the middle of the path. It was no weasel this time, trying to thwart his advance. Then Sam heard a familiar voice:

"Fire! Fire, I say, boy! When in hell, keep walking. Just don't stand there in harm's way, acting so bumfuzzled!" It was Uncle Amos, the armadillo.

"Fine, I say you grew up just fine, a fine figure of a dragon, Bohdan. Bigger than yer dear mama and almost as big as your good ole pappy," said Uncle Amos with watery eyes, and it was not from the smoke. "Do I know you?" said Bohdan, taken aback by the mention of his parents. "Well, I should think so, son. I have been around a long time, up and under da roots of this here place. And now, boy, you must do as your mama once did, and get dar to the source of this fire and put it out. But oh, Lordy has it spread, and I hope we are not too late. I would have come sooner, but I had to get them dar beavers up the crick to build a dam and finish this once and for all. They are an industrious people, but boy howdy does their delightful conversation drag on and on, and ya can't rush a beaver when they are taking pride in der work. Now we'd better move up yonder a bit before…"

Before he could finish, a large burning branch broke off above them and interrupted Uncle Amos. Bohdan turned, and with a swing of his tail, slapped it away just in time before it could harm them-or so they thought. On the ground before them was Mim's red scarf, but no Mim.

They hastily searched the path and called and called, but there was no Mim. Staying any longer would have been the death of them, and Henry asked for his scarf and tenderly tucked it under his hat on his head. Uncle Amos felt their sorrow, too, but knew there was no time to lose. "It breaks the heart. He was a good bird. He was a brave bird to face each day, despite his fears. His cheerful words will be missed; ALL of his ongoing words will be severely missed. I was counting on the sound of his voice to keep us together when we might not be able to see through this smoke, but now we must not tarry here but go on. Now, grab my tail, boy, as youngin's do crossing the path, while we try to stay on it. We cannot let Mim or these trees die in vain. No, sir, we will not!" said the impassioned armadillo, turning to Sam.

Sam grabbed Uncle Amos by the tail, and Henry grabbed onto Sam's fur, and Bohdan stretched his neck over them, extinguishing any flames that continued to mar their way. "We must get ahead of the flames before they spread to the petrified wood. There is evil in the air, and the wind threatens to blow this to the Sequoyah," said Uncle Amos gravely.

The party slowly moved forward, struggling to stay on the path through the smoke. Through the dark fumes, the sound of sharp whistles could then be heard. "Ostap! My boy! My boy! Follow the clear chirps of the cardinals, all is not lost yet. We still have hope, and that becomes as much as you make of it. Time to take a little faith and move a mountain of fire… plus, I no longer have to worry about lighting my pipe," chuckled Uncle Amos with a good-natured wink. "We will find out who is to blame now!" roared Bohdan with renewed vigor, clearing a swath of fire from their path.

# Chapter 19

## LIGHTNING THE LOAD

# The Runt Oak

Ian looked out of his bedroom window. It was a clear night, and he stared at the stars, thinking that somewhere in this big universe, there was a little dog which needed him. All the memories of his time with Sam came flooding back, like a dam which burst in his heart. He remembered when his Uncle Jake brought him home. His dad was against the dog staying in the house, but his mom had allowed Ian to sneak the little pup into his room.

After a while, it was an accepted part of the daily household routine to be careful each time they used the bathroom upstairs, since Sam would cuddle up next to the door wanting companionship. Ian remembered every little toy he bought for Sam, each one still stored in his room. He remembered every little vet visit, and the time he thought he was going to lose him to some affliction he could not pronounce, and the medication he had to give Sam religiously, which he also could not pronounce. Then there was every moment spent with him sharing the books, movies, and the assorted food off his plate he was not supposed to give him- the human food Sam liked most. Ian took every memory and assigned them to the multitude of stars he was currently looking at.

Lost in a trance, it seemed as if the stars had moved and come closer. It was as if the stars wanted to join the source where he gave them meaning, his heart. As the stars came closer, they became brighter, until Ian realized that they really were coming closer. The closer they came, they appeared to pulsate in intensity. They were not only coming closer, but he could detect them moving in loops, and something else, more of them, became visible. These were not stars.

# Lightning The Load

Eventually, one of the bright travelers came up against the windowpane. It was then joined by a score of others, and they were beating up against the window. These strange little points of illumination were fireflies, or as they call them down South, lightning bugs. The thunder of intent within Ian followed their flashes of lightning, and he felt compelled to open the window.

Ian opened the window. In no time, his room was filled with the pulsating bugs. It reminded Ian of his Aunt Lucinda, who kept Christmas lights up all year round. Before Ian knew it, his room then reminded him of the disco ball his Uncle Jake had in his den, which Jake considered a prized conversation piece.

Ian, being careful not to harm them, walked around; however, avoiding them became increasingly difficult with their growing numbers. Ian then started to tickle all over as the lightning bugs landed on him. Ian not only felt tickled by them, but it was as if they were trying to tell him something. Looking around, he noticed they were no longer by the window of his room, but had concentrated at the bedroom door. They wanted out, and not by the window, and they wanted Ian to follow them.

Ian gently brushed some off the doorknob and opened up the door. Once the door opened, the lightning bugs all went through in a swarm of light, hovering by the stairs like a carnival at night, waiting for Ian to follow. The lights in the house had not been on since his mom was not home. This evening, Vivian had gone to a bunko party-something Vivian just did out of habit now, because that is what women in this small town did and gave her an odd sense of normality. Ian did not need to turn any lights on, though, and this was far from anything normal; all he needed to do was follow these lights onward. Going downstairs, the bugs led him to the kitchen and the backyard door.

# The Runt Oak

Opening the backyard door, the bugs flooded out and then broke off into two separate groups. One group went to the outside water faucet, and the other group went to… the little oak. When Ian walked towards the tree to inspect, the group from the water faucet came and surrounded him and brought his attention back to the faucet. Standing confused in front of the faucet and what they might expect of him, Ian could smell the scent of brush burning again. "Great, another noisy night," thought Ian to himself, since the Fergusons cared more about the beer, they would drink than the brush they felt they had to burn.

Despite the protest of the lightning bugs, Ian walked over to peer across the fence at his bothersome neighbors, only to find they were not burning anything. Where was the smell of this smoke coming from? Looking through the bugs that buzzed around him, he looked at the other group by the little oak and noticed smoke coming from out under the tree as it swirled about their moving lights. The little oak was on fire! Ian then did not need the bugs to tell him to go back to the faucet, and ran to the faucet and hooked up the garden hose. Ian sure wished his Uncle Jake was around to help and then even thought to himself, "did dad finally show up to follow through on burning that little tree down? Nah… his dad never followed through on his promises," and Ian managed a fanatical laugh, which he really needed at the moment.

Turning the faucet on, Ian dragged the hose to the tree, and it seemed oddly to require little effort. Getting to the tree, he noticed the smoke was coming from the hole under the tree. Ian then noticed no water was coming out. "You have to be kidding me. This freaking cheap hose is kinking up again," said Ian, about to go back and check where the water flow was being pinched off. To his amazement, looking back, the hose was floating above the ground courtesy of the lightning bugs, which were also in the process of removing the kink. A blast of water shot out and drew Ian's attention back to the smoking hole under the tree. Whatever was causing the fire, the water was doing little to stop it, and the smoke became only worse.

Ian, with the hose in hand, walked back to the faucet to see if he had really fully opened it. Before he could get halfway there, he felt a yank, and the bugs started dragging him back to the oak. These bugs were unusually strong, but these bugs also increased in number. More fireflies apparently had poured out from under the smoking hole, and the next thing Ian knew, they were dragging the hose along with Ian into the hole!

Ian fought from being pulled in and dropped the hose, but in doing so, it got tangled around his leg. With his leg wrapped in the hose, he started getting pulled into the hole. As his feet started disappearing into the smoke and lights of the bugs all around him, he awaited to get crushed into a hole there was no way his body could fit into… and then just like that, his body had broken through in a state of free-falling. The lightning bugs were still about him, as if he was in an hourglass surrounded by light. It was no longer the bugs pulling him forward, but something much more. Ian felt warm and could smell an assortment of what appeared to his human scent to be vegetation. The earth mixed with the sweet scents of vegetation and the acrid smell of the smoke. The lightning bugs diminished, but wait… they had not diminished but only lost their illuminated placement in a light-up head which he was moving upwards towards.

Ian then felt a hard jerk. The hose which he was straggled to had snagged on a giant root. While suspended in this traveling force of energy, he could then notice more roots about him. He had to undo the hose from the root somehow or he would surely be torn apart. Ian reached for the snagged hose, and putting his hand on the root to stabilize himself, he felt a burst of energy. Ian's grip froze on the root as he was gripped in shock. Caught in this frozen moment of heat, he felt a deep voice vibrate in his consciousness say, "Find Sam. Follow the path on the other side from where you came out.

# The Runt Oak

Find Sam. Follow your fears, for they will guide you to your resolution. Put out the fire. Find Sam. Put out the fire." With that, Ian's grip came undone along with the hose, and he was sent racing back upwards. The bright light ahead, which he had seen, was quickly getting dark, and then all went black.

Blinded by light, Ian opened his eyes. As he came to, he removed his hand from his face and realized he was lying on his back. Above, sunlight was shining down on him through a canopy high above. Lifting himself on his elbows in a puddle of mud, his eyes followed this network of branches down to an enormous trunk of an oak tree. Standing himself up, Ian stood face to face with the same majestic oak which had once greeted Sam. Ian had arrived in the realm with no name. Ian was now in a world which held the one name he was looking for: Sam.

# Chapter 20

# FRIEND OR FEAR

# The Runt Oak

**M**uch like Sam, Ian started to investigate, and it was hard not to start with the grandeur of the Grandfather Oak. He walked around the trunk of this magnificent tree, unable to look past it. It was incredible, but also very familiar in an odd way, almost like home, but not. Every step he took, he heard a squish; it was his socks and they were soaking wet... As he made his way to the rear of the tree, he was yanked backwards and proceeded to fall face-first into the ground. Now, it all came back to him, the lightning bugs, the smoke from under the little oak in his yard, and the unreal journey which apparently ended him up here.

Ian turned on the ground to get up and became aware of the hose still wrapped around his ankle, which caused his fall, and something else- he felt a voice while close to the ground. The roots of the Grandfather Tree were reiterating the same messages he heard when he was traveling through the subterranean portal… "Follow the path on the other side from where you come out. Follow your fears, for they will guide you. Put out the fire. Find Sam. Put out the fire!"

"FIND SAM," Ian did not know what this all meant, but hearing the name Sam was all that was needed to be said. He was at the rear of the tree, but there was no way he was going to go forward. Ian noticed the hose was wrapped around his ankle and the trunk, holding him back from where he came. The hose, how did the hose get so long? Everything was strange enough, and he had no time for logical repose, but only to find Sam. The first thing that needed to be done was to get the hose unwrapped around his leg.

Ian stood up and, reaching down, untangled the hose about his ankle. He felt a gush of pressure released into the hose. The hose was still pumping water from his house! Ian thought to himself that his mom would not be too happy with the water bill. Where was the end of the hose where all the water was coming out? Retracing his steps around the trunk, he saw the hole he had come out of and the hose still inserted there, but could not yet find the end as the hose ran in the other direction to the rear of the tree. With the hose in hand, Ian followed it around the opposite direction to the rear and saw it trail off into a grove of elm trees. Hand over hand, he grabbed the hose as it led him into the elms. Leaving the giant oak behind, Ian held onto the hose, making his way under the foliage of trees, which then opened up to a grand sight.

Before him was not only the end of the hose gushing with water, it laid on a wide paved road that went straight into the distance. There was something else; it was lined with trees- cedar trees! Cedar trees, his arch-nemesis from his countless battles against asthma. Ian wanted to turn back, but he also wanted to find Sam. With trepidation, Ian picked up the running hose and walked forward onto the paved road. After all the exertion since his arrival, he awaited for the wheezing which he was sure would come, being in the presence of the cedars which lined both sides. The wheezing, though never came, but what did come were voices. The voices were coming from the cedar, and they knew who he was!

"Take a deep breath," said one voice, and Ian felt a need to approach one of the cedars where the feeling originated. Ian felt a coming together, as if a puzzle was fitting itself together:

"We knew you would come along, Ian, and like you, we were afraid. We were afraid of facing the guilt for our role in a grand design, which is beyond even our comprehension. For even though we were the first trees of the Creator, we know no more than the last, for time moves in a circle, and that circle has brought you back around to us. All those moments of fear when you could not breathe in our presence were just a prelude to this moment- and this finale.

"It is all one, Ian, and now you are prepared to face the fumes which threaten our realm. Your lungs are strong, like the roots of a weathered tree. Only you can endure the storm by having passed through it before it came. We apologize for the affliction as the precursor, and are proud to be the resolution. It is done while it is happening. Take the hose and follow the road. Find both our salvations, and find the Son of Vovk. Find Sam, and Ian… just breathe, just breathe," implored voices coming from the cedar.

Ian felt embraced with comfort, but also reached out with a purpose. He picked up the hose, and the sunlight on the water from the hose sparkled off the wet stones of the road. If these were the first trees of the Creator, then it was only fitting- because this road reminded him of his books, and the first roads of Rome, and the Appian Way. Ian still could not wrap his head around why the hose could still provide water, or even more fantastically, its unending length. Then again, it was no longer wrapped around his leg and was no longer that much of a chore to pull along.

As Ian went up the road, he noticed something strange, which is stating a lot after all he had witnessed so far. The road at times would seem to shift, going at angles, but when he would look back, the hose was in a straight line going back on a straight road. Words in the wind then rustled through the cedars as if to say, "life is about perspective, and though the path ahead may seem to go in different directions, the right direction never alters. It does not allow one to get tied up in the past."

An endless supply of water, a hose with no end, TALKING TREES, and an ever-shifting road which would remind him it did not shift… perfect sense, huh? But then again, so much of our lives offers just as much solace, because there is so much information we do not know and have little control over. So, in retrospect, hold on to the hose, go forward, and find Sam, was actually more than fair compensation. Keep it simple, get it done, and let the chips fall as they may.

The cedar people kept Ian company, and unlike the whispering pines, were supportive. One of the main things they did was make him laugh. Laughter truly is the best medicine, and it made Ian realize why his favorite heroes benefited from a sidekick to curb the stress. As Ian went along, he heard such comments as, "Who is that?" and responses as "one of the 'people' people." Then there was the "does he always dress like that?" which another Cedar responded, "I would think so, he is evergreen like us." Granted, it was very dry humor, but Ian learned to appreciate this type of humor from all the late-night broadcasts of the BBC, which his PBS channel played on Saturday nights. By the way, what is red and sits in a corner? A parked double-decker bus.

Ahead was no double-decker bus, but there was red on the horizon which rose far above two decks- and it was not parked but moving. Ian could see a red glow above the tree lines, and the sky was very dark with smoke. It was the same smoke he had smelled in his yard, and it seemed he had found its origins. As Ian walked on, he noticed that the road he was on was slowly diminishing.

Eventually, the cobblestone road fragmented, till there was no road at all. In front, he now saw a field of sunflowers, which gave off a tinge of orange as it meshed with the red on the horizon. The red on the horizon was a forest on fire. Ian itched as he broke through the sunflowers, leading the hose behind him. The sunflowers towered above him. They seemed to face the truth of the sun as if for help from the artificial heat in front of them.

The next thing he knew, Ian found himself falling down an embankment he did not see in his line of sight, while he too was preoccupied searching for truth. Ian finally felt thankful for the hose, as it saved him from falling down into the ravine below. Holding onto the hose, he propelled himself off the sides of the embankment, reaching the ground floor. It was a shallow flowing river which had formed this escarpment, and standing now on the edge of the river saw pecan trees. He saw pecan trees… walking!

"We got this, mate!" shouted one of the pecan trees, as they were laden with buckets of water on the back of their bent trunks. The pecans were in tight formation, and one finally paused long enough to adjust a bucket sliding off him to tell Ian he was needed at the far end of the forest. "Where is the far end?" pleaded Ian, looking at an immense pine forest which reminded him of the pines behind his house, where he never knew ended or started either.

"What is the holdup?" shouted another voice, and Ian looked around, trying to find which tree might have said that." "Down here, boy!" said a voice, and looking down, he saw a tree lizard. "You can't just drag that contraption through here; you are going to trip up my crew. The sooner we get this taken care of, the sooner I can direct my home back to my home. Take that hose back down to the river and run it across that sandbar to the other side, would you?" said the tree lizard with authority far bigger than its size. Ian wanted to spray the little loudmouth with his hose, but had dealt with such outbursts before when his father was still around. Arguing would do no good, and even trying to find a compromise would have done more bad than good. Time was of the essence, and this fire did not have the patience Ian did.

Ian moved the hose back to the river bottom, him going back and the stalwart faces of the pecans going forward. When he made it back, he found one of the many sandbars which cut across and dragged the limitless hose to the opposite side of the pecan trees' formation. Ian still did not have any notion of where the far side of the forest could be. Overhead, it suddenly became dark.

# Friend Or Fear

At first, Ian thought it was a cloud, or worse, a new fire that had erupted from behind, but both were not the case. Looking up, he heard the cries of an assortment of birds of every shape and color. The dark cloud was a massive flock going in a hurry. From this dark rolling layer of feathers, he saw what appeared to be a green banner unfurling and coming towards him. As this descending green flag approached him, it turned out to be a mockingbird wearing an emerald green scarf, "Eh eh Ian, fa fah follow us. We are uh uh on our way to the fa fah far end of the pines. Ha huh hurry bah before your sa sah Sam becomes a ha hawt hotdog!"

# Chapter 21

# A PLACE TO BE A HERO

# The Runt Oak

The tail end of the mockingbird's green scarf fluttered from sight as the bird returned to the mass of birds flying high above. Ian was now moving to the right of the line of industrious pecan trees and moving in the right direction. The landscape before him was an even field, which seemed to cradle the immense pine forest that was on fire. Looking back, the ever extending hose was coming along smoothly enough, and the pecans seemed to have done an admirable job because the fire was noticeably less. Looking ahead was a different story altogether. The glowing red on the fringes of the pine forest was rising like some demonic dance. The flames towered on the horizon, turning the atmosphere into an oven. Ian could hear the crackling wood and, even worse, the cries of the trees. The smoke from the ongoing fire then enveloped his way and was getting thicker.

As the fumes burned his lungs, Ian kept track of the long line of birds, which seemed as never-ending as the length of the hose he held in his hand. Ian had felt this strain on his lungs before from the many asthma attacks of his youth, and though at first it jolted his nerves, this was not something he was unaccustomed to. While most would have given up, Ian knew he was more than capable of enduring the smoke, but for how long? The birds above then made a gradual descent, slowly towards where the pines stopped, and a vague hill to the right could be seen, clouded in vapors.

The ground in front of Ian was aglow from the fire, casting shadows of hundreds of birds flowing across it, pointing his way. Ian felt as if he was moving in one of the old shadow candle boxes his mom had in the dining room. When Sam was a pup, he would chase the shadows on the wall when Ian's mom would light the candles, sending the assorted shapes of stars in motion. Ian missed Sam dearly, and one cannot filter the happiness from sorrow when the emotions of loss collide. In his mind, Ian now remembered holding onto Sam when the dog was sick on that cold table in the waiting room at the vet's. Ian remembered all the days his mom dropped him off to see Sam, as the little dog had an IV in him. Sam pulled through, but the thought of seeing Sam lying on the ground, helpless again, sent a shock of urgency through him. "Sam? Where are you, Sam?" agonized Ian, and he started to run faster towards the glowing rim of what seemed like an orb of fire licking the pines in the distance. Ian ran faster, the hose bruising his legs as it slapped up against him with his ever-increasing pace.

Meanwhile, in the roaring furnace of the pines, Sam was converging towards the very destination that Ian was now headed. Ostap darted in and around the path as Sam and his party moved through the burning pines, following his directions through unfamiliar places, which would veer on and off the deteriorating path. "We are getting close to the edge. Take heart. We must stop this fire before it spreads over into the Sequoyah," shouted the cardinal. All around, Sam could now feel the pines, which no longer whispered. Instead of hateful spite, he only heard words begging for forgiveness. He also heard something else, accountability, as the pines would say their individual names in these acts of contrition. Henry was now seated on top of Bohdan's head, feeling what the dragon's eyes could see for him. Sam was shocked by how fast an armadillo could move, seeing Uncle Amos resemble a little tank plowing ahead. Sam was even more shocked that he could still keep up, but like Ian with the fumes- for how long? Thankfully for Sam, his breed was rather small, and being close to the ground helped him avoid most of the smoke as it rose upward. Thankfully for all, was the presence of Bohdan was leading the way, crashing through the fallen pines which might have blocked their path, and blowing a steady stream of frost into the flames.

It was becoming hard to see with all the smoke from the fire and the extinguished flames from the efforts of Bohdan, when suddenly the space cleared. Sam, trying to keep up, sped past Bohdan and felt as if he had hit a wall. Stepping back, Sam saw he had run straight into a stone relief of a whale, the same giant whale fossil which had once marked their exit from the petrified hill. There too was the Sequoyah up on the hill of mist, sentinels of the ancient realm at the brink of their possible destruction.

Then Sam became puzzled, "Where are the sycamores, for I do not recall seeing them and those are the Sequoyah ahead?" "I did not notice them either, but then again, they were too afraid to even speak and make their presence known before," said Henry feeling sad. "I am afraid they are no more and were permanently replaced by a new reality. Yes, it is sad but can happen when you no longer are able to challenge lies. Their silence sealed their faith and now they exist in an illusion forever," stated Uncle Amos. "Yes, when you are no longer able to reject the illusion, over time you accept them as truth. You lose who you are. I got out of my cave of illusion in the nick of time," said Bohdan grimly.

They had made it to the edge of the pines, and turning behind him was the building fire, which they would have to stop. To say 'they would have to stop' would be stating it rather loosely. This daunting task would fall onto the frost dragon, but as it is with friends and them being an extension of each other, Bohdan, their friend, now had something good that was real- something he would fight to protect. A nomad from Vovk's people, a blind squirrel, and an outcast dragon were showing they belonged in this world or any other.

# A Place To Be A Hero

As they stood with their backs to the petrified hill, they could see flakes of ash drift down after the mist over the Sequoyah extinguished the blown sparks on the wind. These sparks were like advanced scouts for the army of fire, which was getting closer and closer. Once the fire would ignite the edge in full force, it would be futile to expect the mist to prevent the Sequoyah's impending doom. Bohdan, though, needed time to replenish his frost after the arduous ordeal of reaching the edge. The stressed party waited as the frost dragon regained his strength. Henry was about to say something, not being able to control his fear as he felt the heat of the fire burning closer, but then felt a low voice tell him that Bohdan could not be rushed. Bohdan himself was desperately trying to rush his recovery, and his anxiety was not helping him regain his frost. In this crackling silence before the storm, voices could then be heard in song. It was the female Sequoyah from across the hill which had ushered his name before. A very moving and brooding song filled the air.

*"Fire and ice from the north*

*Arrived regal Drakon and Drakaina*

*Peace and happiness they sought*

*Removed from hunters' mania*

*An egg of love tenderly brought*

*For hope, leaving behind hysteria*

*Hail, little Bohdan's icy mouth."*

Bohdan was moved by the song of the Lady Sequoyah and felt a noble sensation that rose deep within his core. Henry then heard the low voice again; it was Anton. "Hold on, little brother." Henry held on as Bohdan expanded in size, and his violet scales started to attain a pulsating shade of blue. The frost dragon inhaled, tilting his head back, and Henry held on for dear life. From Bohdan's icy mouth, a blast of cold erupted in force towards the fire, and it was none too soon as the main vanguard of flames had arrived. Steam enveloped the edge of the pines as the frost dragon went to work. The fire could not match the ferocity of the dragon's cold charge, and dwindled in a futile retreat with no escape.

Then something odd happened. Bohdan started to falter, and the stream of frost became broken. Henry yelped and felt a sharp sting, which was joined by others. "Well, I'll be a skunk in daylight. We need to fall back to the safety of the petrified rocks… FIRE ANTS!" shouted Uncle Amos, and he rolled on the parched earth. All over had appeared fire ants, which, having crept up, suddenly unleashed their unified bites. Each time they would fall dead from under the cold scales of Bohdan, more would crawl under and do their devious work. Sam jumped on a rock and instinctively started barking uncontrollably. Sam hated when this emotive tick came over him, but Uncle Jake simply said it was just a case of LDS- Little Dog Syndrome, that irritating impulse of barking which smaller dog breeds inherently did. The fire then gained ground, ground with pines on it, and regrouped, advancing even stronger than before with a vengeance. Ill winds of change, and what had seemed so hopeful was now going up in flames.

Sam hopped from one petrified rock to another, fending off the demented tiny ants, when he then felt things brush past his fur. Birds had arrived, hundreds of birds. Sparrows, wrens, robins, jays, every bird one could think of had flown in, and then on a rock next to him, he heard a familiar voice… it was Mim! "I ha huh heard you ba bah barking, barking and ba barking from all the wa way up there in da the sky, and ya you said I ta tah talk too ma much nonsense… sasa Sam!" said Mim. Sam was overjoyed and knocked Mim off the rock and licked him.

As the two friends rolled around laughing, a voice fluttered above them. "Tha there will ba bah be plenty of tah time for that lah later, Mimyr. That is na nah not in the pa proper pa pah pecking order for now. We ha have wa wah work to do!" said a female mockingbird. "Mimyr?" said Sam, as he rolled himself off of Mim. "My sa sasa sister, la lah Lucinda, and I can fa fah fly now! She is rah right, tah time for that la lah later," said Mim as he joined his feather cohorts. The birds were going after the fire ants! Bohdan then regained his composure and started finding a steady stream of frost, but the fire had gained a stingy foothold.

Maybe if the birds had gotten there sooner, the battle would not be raging so precariously, but they needed the mist above the Sequoyah to dampen their feathers in order to endure the heat on their arrival. This was going to be a hard fight, and any tip of the balance could ultimately decide the outcome. From the smoke, Ostap's red plumage appeared as if he had flown down a chimney, and with a sharp, clear cry, shouted, "Who or what is that?"

It was Ian! Sam suddenly went into another fit of LDS, overcome by joy. "My boy, my boy, Sam!!!" shouted Ian. "Is Ian another one of Vovk's people?," exclaimed Henry, to which Uncle Amos replied, "not rightly, he is 'people' people, and he needs to now unload that water pistol at the fire," and with that the armadillo latched onto the hose and redirected Ian's attention and aim at the fire. That one little tip of the balance happened with that tip from the armadillo. After another grueling hour, the fire was put out… the day was won!

Since the battle is won, the fruits of victory should be shared in full circle. It was not just a frost dragon, the contribution of birds, or the timely arrival of Ian, which ultimately saved the day- but something else. No matter how small the role that is played, all the participants of an outcome are significant. History often leaves out what it considers minor roles, the small people, but those 'small' people are a crucial part of the grand macrocosm. On the edge of these pines were also found the refugees of strife. The ones nobody wants, but those in their wanting to belong. Huddled and pressed up against the small space afforded them, in the undergrowth below their towering neighbors, were the hackberries. Places others ignored, but they still found value.

Yes, those resilient people who endure no matter the stones of indifference which are cast their way. If it had not been for their steadfast determination, those on the ground would have never been able to escape the heat which tried to outflank our heroes from below. The victory won that day was a testament to acceptance and a refusal to be cast aside, the immense value for who and what you are. The hackberries held their own and held the line for others. Their thorny branches, which they share with the rose, might not have been able to deter the flames, but it was what bloomed within them that mattered most.

# Chapter 22

# REUNITED IN THE INNER CIRCLE

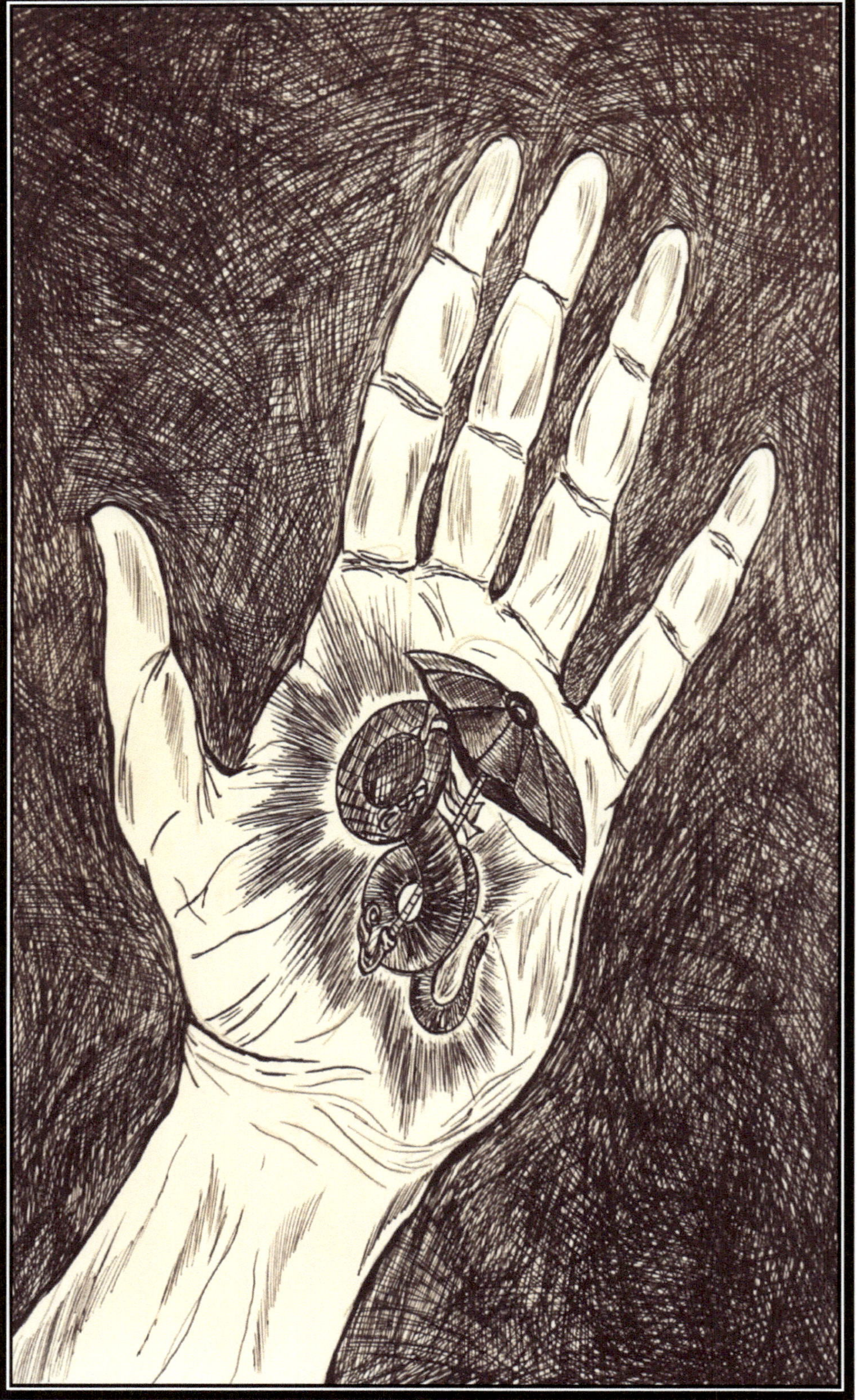

# The Runt Oak

The birds were dealing with the aftermath. It was especially heartbreaking to see the little wrens in such a state, and even their turf war rivals, the tufted titmice, showed them empathy. Then there were the brutish blue jays who took an interest in the broken state of their smallest comrades, as the hummingbirds, one jay cradling a little fellow, saying, "Come, little warrior, you are no worse for wear." Something had definitely changed in this realm. There was now a self-awareness extending past the self to the well-being and respect of others, for one has to acknowledge oneself to appreciate the individual that also resides in others. The companions viewed this scene and had been contemplating what laid deep within them too when Uncle Amos finally broke the silence above the dim of Bohdan's steady breathing.

"Let's get up and go to the Sequoyah, for I feel Anton the elder a callin'," said Uncle Amos, as he lit his pipe on one of the remaining embers from the fire. Bohdan, who had been sitting down with his back to his friends for quite some time, finally rose and turned to the misty hill of the ancient trees. "Let there be no fatigue on the day of victory, and I am curious to meet these 'Sequoyah'?"

Ian was amazed by all he had seen, but if he had known Bohdan when Sam had first met him, he would have been more so now. It was still Bohdan with his childlike transparency, but there was a new energy and a regal bearing which the trial by fire had brought forth, which made the dragon feel much bigger than even his physical size.

As the gathered victors stepped aside for the broad strides of the frost dragon, Sam jumped into Ian's arms. "Oh, Sam, I missed you so much. I never thought I would find you again, and now I find you in a place I never would have imagined existed," said Ian, full of emotion. "I am so happy to see you, too!" said Sam. At that, Ian dropped Sam in shock, "You can talk?" "Well, of course, he can talk. Aren't you a talkin' too, boy?" said Uncle Amos as they followed Bohdan up the petrified path to the Sequoyah. Seeing his friends head up the path, Mim finished attending to his folk and joined his old compatriots.

Walking up the hill, Henry turned to the hovering voice of Mim, who was flying around the party singing a song of victory, "We thought you were done for in the fire, and how is it you can finally fly, brother?" Mim perched himself next to Henry on the tail of Bohdan where he was seated, and explained, "I ma must ba bah blacked out when that da dah the ba branch fell, bah but luckily this ma mah mole came out of duh the ground and fa fah found me. Na nah not so easy to sah see a ga gah grey bird lying in ah ash uh uh hu unconscious," said Mim.

"But how is it that you can fly, and what's up with the name Mimyr?" said Sam, happily walking again alongside Ian as he had done so many times during one of their walks back home. "Da duh ma mole took me to mah my kind, and to ma my suh surprise there was ma mah my sa sasa sister Lucinda. I tah thought I had la lost my fa fah family forever bah but no. Sa seeing her fa fah fly and ah alive, I just fa fah flew. Ha happiness is the ba bah best ma medicine I ga gah guess," said an exuberant Mim. Bohdan turned his tail where seated his friends to his face, "Mimyr? Do not recall hearing such a name in this neck of the woods before. That is an Old World name… very fine, very fine indeed," he said with approval. "Ya yah Ma mah Mimyr, sah seems that is ma my fa fah full na na name. Ja jah just call me ma mah Mim," said Mim, a little embarrassed. "Absolutely, brother," said Henry, and then the entire party said "Mimyr" and started laughing- all but Ian, who had yet to stop smiling, but was still too astonished to take part in a conversation between animals being led by a dragon.

Upon reaching the misty hill of the mystic trees, the victors were led to the inner circle of the Sequoya. As Ian looked at the towering ancient trees for the first time, he marveled at their noble stature rising to the clouds. Ian then could have sworn he saw, for a passing moment, reliefs of what appeared to be faces of Lords and Ladies in the trunks of the 13 trees. The faces reminded him of his books and the kings and queens of old. They had the same stoic expression about them, which the burden of rule leaves its toll, but these were also filled with a compassion that one can only feel in person. As the saying goes, sacrifice is a sign of nobility, and their regal bearing had endured much. Gathered in the center of the circle, feelings of gratitude and happiness filled the space. After the vibrations of emotions settled, Anton spoke.

"First, we must address the most urgent of matters, for one must not be lazy and betray all the hard work which made this possible. The last leaves are as important as the first, for they are where the blooms are found. Amos, have the beavers built the dam as I instructed you?"

"Yes, Anton, it is built as you advised," said Uncle Amos.

"Good, for the ice of Bohdan now melts, and the water will find its way to the treacherous Deadwood Tree. Water is an element of life (at this, Uncle Amos reached over and whispered to Ostap, "how else do you think Anton could get the pecans to move by the river?), and it will wash away the dead roots of that accursed manipulator and its insatiable jealousy and need for control," said Anton, and there was a low hum of approval from the circle of trees.

# Reunited In The Inner Circle

"Now, Eva, come forward," said Anton, and a female cardinal flew into the inner circle. Eva landed next to Ostap, who had also come forward.

"Go now and find your winged brethren who have suffered in the fight and lead them to ferns. The dew of enlightened tears has found their release, and their innocence has triumphed over their former petty distractions. They will heal the wounded. Let them heal in the pools under them, for their nurturing depths are deeper than their shallow appearance," said Anton, and the two cardinals bowed low with their tail feathers spread out, and then flew to Anton's bidding.

"Bring forth her Ladyship," said Anton, and entering the circle came a mole with a glowing light gently in his paws. The mole walked towards Sam and his friends, handing this precious item to Ian. Ian opened and cupped his hands to receive what the mole had, and as his hands became warm and tingly, it revealed Gloria the glow worm. "Hold her up so she may see the recipients of her grace, but do be careful," said Anton. Ian carefully held up the glow worm, and Gloria lowered her parasol as she spoke to the companions:

"For your bravery, Ian, I give back your beloved Sam, for his service here is done. There is more, but you will find this out when you return to your world, for the gifts are with you even now."

"For your gallant contributions, Mimyr, I give you the gift of new songs which this realm has not heard for many years from better times. Teach them to your kind, and repeat them during the solace of spring nights so the happiness is never lost again.

"For you, Henry… well, look about you," and the squirrel's eyes opened wide. Henry could see, and all he could say was "awe, brother", as he looked at his friends and the world for the first time.

The mole then gestured to Ian to return to his care, Gloria. The mole delicately took her in his paws and walked back out of the circle.

Then Anton spoke again and said, "Behold!" The light increased in the inner circle, and looking up, the companions noticed that the sun above had been joined by another sun. This sun seemed to move, and then it eclipsed before their eyes. Slowly, the darkness left this sun as it seemed to change shape, moving down from the sky, accompanied by a blue moon. Then the orbed shapes became clearer, revealing it had been a dragon embracing another dragon. "Mother… father!" said Bohdan with his voice breaking with emotion. "Yes, Bohdan, your parents. They were exiled from our land after they brought you here, but your deeds today will prove your kind is good, a very good thing. It was your mother who had put out a fire many years ago that caused a great flood, and they wrongly blamed the fire on your father. This was the first sign of the Deadwood's corrupted existence, but no one would listen to our suspicions. I kept you close, Bohdan, knowing with patience you would prove our judgment right. And now, it is time for Ian and the Son of Vovk to return to their world."

With those words, there were many heartfelt goodbyes, but not for Sam's friends who had joined on this quest, who, along with Ian, would accompany each other one last time on their way back to the Grandfather Tree. Before leaving, something was done which had not been done on the misty hill for many ages- each member of the party gave all 13 trees a hug, though when leaving, no one was still quite sure which one had been Anton.

Down the petrified road, they reached the edge of the pines, who were now simply just the pine people, and there were no whispers but clarity. There was something else, too; a rather daunting river had formed from all the melting frost that Bohdan had spent in the battle against the fire. This was nothing like the shallow river which

Ian had crossed, and even Uncle Amos was lost for answers. Their perplexing dilemma on how to cross the strong currents was soon rectified before Bohdan could spread his wings and say "hop on". A small company of pecan trees appeared to help them bridge the icy river, led by a tired tree lizard who said, "Guess I won't be getting my home home on time after all."

Crossing the bridge, they looked across the wide field which Ian had initially taken, and Ian turned to Uncle Amos as if to ask if he was heading in the right direction. Uncle Amos burst into laughter, "Don't search across the field, boy. They say the people of Vovk and the 'people' people often bond with those they are most alike, and that seems to hold true. Just like Sam, you are bumfuzzled. Don't search across. No, search in the field before you… The hose, boy, look for the hose." Sure enough, there was the hose leading straight back into the horizon.

One could really not blame Ian for forgetting. After all, just the fact that an armadillo was talking to you would be enough bumfuzzling to last a lifetime. Off they went, following the hose, retelling all they had seen and done, and most of all, all they felt. They made their way across the shallow lower river where the imprints of Ian's last walk were still present. Ian grabbed the hose, which was still hanging from the embankment, to climb up, when he then felt a nudge. It was Bohdan, and he lowered his long, sturdy neck as a ladder for all to traverse the sandy ledge. While crossing over the ledge, protruding roots gave off vibes of happiness. "Did you feel that?" said Ian to Sam, and Sam thought back in retrospect to his bitter experience at the bottom of the gorge, and smiling said, "Yes, I feel you. They need to put up a sign which says 'Smiles Kept A Coming Ledge'."

After they all had made it across to the top, Bohdan suggested they get on his back this time to avoid the beautiful but itchy sunflowers that encompassed this side of the escarpment- all but

Mim, who hopped, but did not hop, at having a chance to enjoy his new joy for flight. Soaring above the sunflowers, Ian imagined that this is what it must be like to be a bee. And Henry? Overcome with bliss, would never have to imagine again what all now seemed beautiful - looking about in wonder. They then spotted the paved road below, and while they descended to the road, they all heard a soft whining noise which resembled an old organ grinder. It was a flock of cedar waxwings going to… why, of course… the cedar trees lining the road below.

On landing, the companions got off the back of the frost dragon. Bohdan had never been to this part of the realm before, and told them he would fly just a little ahead to satisfy his curiosity and see how far the Grandfather Tree was. It was only after a few minutes that Bohdan came back. "I think it is best to follow the hose. I almost crashed trying to follow that road… it kept changing direction every time I took my eyes off it." Ian laughed, nodding in simple agreement. "That is a good perspective to take, 'don't look too far ahead'. One can never be certain when it's the present that ultimately decides the path," said Uncle Amos. Together they all walked on, as cedar waxwings would come and go, passing berries to each other and them, till there was then a vibration felt from under the road- they were getting close to the Grandfather Tree.

# Chapter 23

# GRIGORIJ

# The Runt Oak

The Colonel paced the floor in his house on the Deadwood Tree. Something was wrong, very wrong, but in all actuality, something had been wrong for some time in his life. Even if he had not been suffering from this sudden, overwhelming feeling of anxiety, he would have been hard pressed to find anywhere to sit, even if he wanted to. There had been so many shifts in his house of late, he no longer could find any security in knowing where his rooms were or could depend on the location of his furniture. Cyrus had not shown up since the day he hatched his evil plan to destroy the Sequoyah, and all that imposed a threat to his control, real or mostly imaginary.

The owl was finding it hard to concentrate. His perspective of the world had been an illusion he had crafted in his own fragile world to begin with, a beginning he was no longer sure of due to all the lies he no longer knew to be true or false. He developed a headache, and it was not just his worries, but something else. No longer able to focus, his eyes turned to a stained glass window which always was behind his desk, even when all within would shift. It was there.

For the first time, he noticed the colors of the stains on the glass actually now cast their light on the surface of his desk. Light was coming through, which never did before, into the dark void where the Deadwood Tree stood, and the light hurt his eyes. Something was not right, not right at all, and he had no one to whom to manipulate their reality to rationalize his own pseudo reality. No Cyrus, no ferrets, and not even one single bug… the Colonel was all alone.

# Grigorij

The Colonel tried to open one of the windows in his house. He did not know why he felt so compelled to do so, but he was now finding it hard to breathe. He needed fresh air, but was too scared to go for a flight, being so unsure of everything around him. The Colonel did not know whom to trust because he could not even trust himself, avoiding his true self for so many years.

Wedged tight from years of disuse, the window proved immovable. The owl's temper then exploded, mad at what he had no clue, and threw a paperweight from his desk at the window in an effort to let fresh air come in. The paperweight only caused a slight crack, and the Colonel then picked up a cane from the corner of the study and bashed the window. Although the glass shattered, the incoming air remained musty and putrid. Looking at the shattered window, he noticed it had been boarded up by driftwood over the years from the outside in order to keep the appearance of a stable exterior for a house never truly intact. He then went to find the door to exit his house, and could not. The house and his mind had shifted so much; he could no longer find his way out.

The Colonel screamed, and crying uncontrollably, took all his remaining energy and threw a chair at the accursed stained glass window, which haunted him. The window shattered, and a flood of light blinded him as he slumped over the edge, exhausted from throwing the chair. His head hanging over the edge of the window, he felt a fresh breeze but also sensed something else- he heard a roaring sound building in the distance. The Colonel twisted his head toward the sound and was stunned by what he saw.

The newfound light revealed a wasted clearing where the Deadwood stood. Gnarled roots and dead vegetation left to rot. On the ground, he saw dead branches, branches which must have once had joy and life, but were used up and then discarded at the base of the dark tree. The Colonel looked at the dead branches and found himself crying again. The branches, as if seeking escape from their ruined lives, began to move away. The Colonel then wanted to leave too, along with the branches, but how are the dead able to move?

The Colonel then realized how they were getting swept away by an increasing stream of water below. As the dead vegetation got carried away with the water, the Colonel could see what lay beyond… a tidal wave of water was approaching swiftly, and it was heading straight for him. Something then clicked in the owl, and he took off flying through the broken stained glass into the light. He could feel the warmth of the sunlight, though he was unable to see clearly in the light. The air of the open sky dried his tears as he flew blindly as fast as he could. He refused to look back, and it was not fear that prevented him, but shame. The Colonel flew till he could fly no more, and once being able to recognize a tree after getting accustomed to the light, landed and rested his body against the trunk, falling asleep.

The Colonel slowly awoke to the sound of a voice. It was a low, comforting voice, and the sun was going down. Everything that had transpired felt like a dream to him. It was not only the events of the great flood which must have washed away his house on the Deadwood Tree, but it seemed his whole past up to that point had been washed clean from his memory. He looked across from the tall tree he was perched on and saw the misty hill of the Sequoyah in the distance. The low voice spoke again and said, "Grigorij." The Colonel felt oddly familiar with the name, and it seemed like an echo which had sometimes reverberated on odd nights coming back to him.

"Grigorij, that is your name. That is your true self. There is no need to be ashamed, but be thankful to be you again," said the soothing, deep voice. "But, but… I am the… the Colonel?" said the unsure owl. "No, the Colonel was one who tried to build a prison around others and yourself, Grigorij. You are now free and must build a new house. The foundation is still within. It is alright. Be

# Grigorij

thankful, child of the moon, it is good to be you, Grigorij. The only reason the Deadwood chose you was because of your fledgling heart, which it thought easy to manipulate, and that big heart was big enough to still have something good left. All is forgiven, for it is better to give than to take. Give yourself back. It was always there."

The owl then dropped his rankings, longing to belong, and no longer the Colonel, Grigorij, softly asked, "Whooo… who is this?" The deep voice responded, but it was hard to make out the name because it was joined by 12 other voices in unison. Nonetheless, it felt good to know his own name- "I am Grigorij, nothing more, but surely nothing less."

# Chapter 24

## SAVE A SEAT FOR ME

# The Runt Oak

It was a long night at the bunko party, since the ladies in town saw it more as an opportunity for gossip than the game in question. The matches would always take forever, between the whispers and the rolling of the dice. Often, Vivian would surrender her place at the table and spend her time with one of the younger school teachers who was more her age. They had gotten to talking, and the schoolteacher, Andrea, told her about a problem she had been having with her kitchen sink. Since Vivian couldn't care less about who lived where, who was related to whom, and how much money they made, she made an early exit with Andrea to take a look at the problem she had with her sink. Her recent success in retrieving her grandmother's ring inspired Vivian, and she thought she might be on a roll and didn't need any dice to make it happen. After hours of effort, Andrea and Vivian still could not fix the plumbing problem, but learned enough to find out how to laugh at what they could not find wrong.

The rest of the evening, Andrea and Vivian talked about many things, and one was Ian. Ian was a student of hers, and laughing, she told Vivian how Ian stated he did not like math because he thought it was an Arabic plot to discredit imagination, since they are responsible for the practicality of mathematics and their religion forbids figurative imagery. This was all Vivian needed to subsequently engage in various conspiracy theories of her own, and Andrea found out where Ian got his imagination. Vivian was about to bring up her theory on the Fergusons and druids, but then noticed how late it was. Saying their goodbyes, Vivian got in her car and drove home. Along the way, she thought about many things, especially how she felt about Ian and hoped he was doing all right, missing Sam. Vivian, finally, drove up to her house and noticed the lights were still on inside.

Vivian walked to the front door, soaking wet from her plumbing education at Andrea's, and as she stepped in and bent down to take off her wet shoes, her face got wet as well. Picking up the source of this moist reception, she held Sam in her arms. "Sam, calm down. I am already soaking wet already, and you better…" and Vivian stopped, taking a moment to process the furry and extremely happy bundle of fur she was holding. "Sam… Sam!" and Vivian cried, and it was then Sam who was getting more wet. Vivian looked up and saw Ian sitting at the dining room table, smiling from ear to ear. "When, how… oh Sam!" said Vivian, trying to hug the dog, which was moving a million miles per hour, being just as excited as her. "Well, I went outside and… there he was," said Ian. His mom looked at him, "Really?" with a smirk on her face. "Uh… really… I was just outside and cleaning up and had the gate open, and the next thing you know, there was Sam," said Ian fumbling for an explanation.

Vivian said nothing, and the smirk became an inquisitive smile. As Ian got up, water dripped from his clothes. "You too?" said Vivian. "Yeah, I was… well, rolling up the hose after noticing someone had left the water on, it seems," said Ian, not trying to make eye contact with his mom. "Then this is what happened… I guess? Well, we all need to get into some dry clothes and get me a towel because Sam is soaking… wait, we have a towel… wait, that is a?" said Vivian, running her fingers through a red scarf that was around Sam's neck. "We were just playing 'Sinbad', and how could Sam be Sinbad without the proper attire… and I thought I would be the monster for a change since I was so happy to see Sam again, and…" stammered Ian. "Upstairs, young skeleton, before your bones catch a cold, while I dry off Sinbad here," said Vivian, as she pointed upstairs with one arm and held Sam in the other.

Ian cleaned up in the upstairs bathroom and walked into his bedroom to find Sam sitting on his bed wagging his tail. Ian flopped onto the bed, and Sam proceeded to jump back and forth over him. "Ok, stop jumping… hey, I mean it. You win, Sinbad, slow down, boy," said Ian, laughing. "It is not jumping, but hopping," corrected Sam. The two friends then started talking about all their adventures and the emotional parting at the Grandfather Tree. Both of them were extremely happy to have had each other when they had to enter the portal again. They talked and talked at a rate which raced as fast as the portal itself.

Ian then stopped and looked at Sam, "You can still talk?" Sam said he wasn't talking, well, at least not in human, "it is you, Ian, you are speaking dog," said Sam with a twinkle in his eye. "Well, I'll be," said Ian, not sure if he had said that in dog or human. "You know what else?" said Sam. Hesitantly, Ian asked what else, expecting to see a dragon poke its head from the upstairs window. "I got that too. You have to be careful when you talk without words, it is almost reading one's mind. It's in the eyes, you know. No, no dragon, and if it was Bohdan, we would probably have two more dragons in the yard. When his parents showed up at the Grandfather Tree, I doubt you could separate them now for the time being," said Sam without saying a word. "Then what else?" said Ian in human speech, being careful with this newfound gift. "Gloria did say we already had her gifts with us, and I approve of the blue wallpaper in this room. You see, I can still see in color," said Sam with his ears perked up for emphasis. "Then I hope you like this simple white blanket," and laughing, Ian shoved Sam under it. With that, a thankful son of Vovk was glad to fall asleep again in a people's bed.

"Ian! Ian, wake up. It's late. Come down here. Are you going to sleep all morning? Your dad is on the phone. He wants to talk to you," yelled his mom from downstairs. Ian had slept late, and at first thought what had happened had been just a dream, till he saw Sam wearing Mim's red scarf and Sam telling him in dog talk, "lazy dog". Ian went downstairs, with Sam trailing behind him. Sam reached the stairs, and they did not scare him anymore. Closing his eyes, he thought of Henry and scampered to the bottom floor. Ian's mom handed the phone over and looked at Sam. "What has gotten into you? Are you a mongoose now?" said Vivian. Sam clearly told her he was a squirrel, but only Ian heard it, smiling at Sam while listening to his father speak.

When Ian was finished talking to his father, he went outside to the back porch to join his mom, drinking her morning coffee. "What did he have to say?" said Vivian. "Oh, the same ole, I guess. How were my grades and such-and-such… and then all he was doing before I could even answer," said Ian. "Nothing about himself, huh? Had the same conversation, but he still grades me," said Vivian, rolling her eyes with a goofy smile to make Ian laugh. Ian grinned and looked out into the yard, and something caught his eye. It was the little runt of an oak tree. "Hey, is it just me, but when I walked out, I noticed the hose seems a little bit longer. Not much more, but… was it always like that… Ian?" Ian came to. "What? Oh, the hose is the same. Must have been your perspective, Mom," said Ian, turning his attention back to the little oak as Sam had joined them on the porch. Ian then noticed what kept drawing him back. It was the little swing his father had put on a branch, which he often blocked out of his mind. The swing was empty and seemed to have always been so. As if Vivian could read his mind in dog talk, she looked at the swing, "he put that up for you, you know? Maybe one day he will find himself… and that swing will no longer be empty."

**THE END**

But then again, that all depends on dimensions. From the strands of red, orange, and yellow, there are worlds of green, blue, and violet. Awe, did I say the color violet? Reminds one of the scales of a frost dragon, which any dog in proximity to the Grandfather Tree could clearly see.

## About the Author

**Raymond Pilarczyk** lives in South Central Texas. Pilarczyk is a modern-day symbolist **artist** known for his large, sprawling paintings, dealing with epic themes ranging from history to mythology. He received his Bachelor of Arts and Bachelor of Fine Arts degrees from the University of Texas at Austin. He completed his Master of Fine Arts degree from the University of Houston. Pilarczyk was mentored by Vincent Mariani, who was a protégé of the noted colorist Josef Albers, the Pop Artist Peter Saul, and the public works artist Luis Jimenez. Pilarczyk has work in private collections in the United States and internationally. Pilarczyk's ancestor, Mathias Pilarczyk, was a captain and bodyguard for the Archduke Maximilian I of Austria, the reigning Emperor of Mexico during the Mexican Revolution, and is a descendant of the Moczygemba family, the founding family of the oldest Polish settlement in the United States, Panna Maria, TX. Other works by Raymond Pilarczyk include **"The Perfect Escape** - *A Creative Discovery of Love."*

*www.rpilar.com*